TURN AROUND

A WOMEN'S FRIENDSHIP FICTION NOVEL

RUNNING WITH FRIENDS
BOOK ONE

CAROLE WOLFE

BLIND VISTA PRESS

www.carolewolfe.com

First Edition

ISBN 978-1-7371985-6-7 (EPUB edition)
ISBN 978-1-968221-00-3 (Paperback edition)
ISBN 978-1-968221-01-0 (Large print paperback edition)

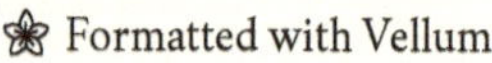 Formatted with Vellum

CHAPTER 1

"**I**t's about time we got a female principal."

Heather Ramsey's lips curved up at her friend's exclamation. She'd known for weeks, but only now did her excitement show.

"It's not a done deal. I sign the contract tomorrow."

But Heather couldn't contain herself. Enthusiasm flushed through her, and she broke into her best running man. Her arms flailed over her head as she picked up her knees, jerking them as high as she could. Her friends laughed and clapped as she took a bow.

"But, yes, you're looking at the next principal of Stadium High School."

"Do not pull out that move at the contract signing. Someone will think you're convulsing." Angela Laing, Esquire, touched her toes.

Heather admired her friend's new purple running shoes that coordinated with the gray-and-purple sport tank and pants. She picked a piece of lint off her faded T-shirt before tightening the drawstring on her husband's old gym shorts. Her first splurge with her significantly larger paycheck would be some new running gear.

Angela added, "Tell us all about your plans while we run."

"We can't start yet." The self-proclaimed leader of the running group, Stacey Friend, checked her watched and scanned the parking lot. "Rachel's not here."

Angela bent into a catcher's squat and looked up at Heather. "What are you going to do when your best friend since kindergarten is late to work? This is why they pay you the big bucks."

Heather pushed her bangs off her forehead. The Texas heat in July was brutal, and they hadn't even started running. Or maybe she'd been worried about this issue before Angela brought it up. She loved Rachel, and all the students adored the English teacher. But Rachel Sato was not known for her punctuality.

"I'll treat her like the rest of the teachers. Be on time or face the consequences. She's usually on time for work, though. Give her a little leeway."

"If someone showed up late to the store this many times, I'd replace them," Stacey said.

With her fists balled on her hips and her chest pushed out, she resembled a superhero preparing for battle. Heather kept that observation to herself, as Stacey wouldn't see the humor in the comparison.

"If Rachel doesn't show up in the next four minutes, I'm going to have to shorten this new running route. My coverage at the store lasts until lunchtime, but I need to check in early to see how Christine is doing."

"It was so nice of you to hire her," Heather said, referring to their mutual childhood friend, Christine Olsen, who had recently moved back to Stadium from Dallas. "This is what she needs until she gets on her feet."

"I really don't think it's good to pop in on her with no warning," Angela said. "We all know she has trust issues."

Stacey shrugged. "I do what I need to do. If I don't watch out for my business, no one will. Speaking of which . . ." Stacey removed one of the two running watches from her arm and held it out to Heather. "Can you try this out and see what you think? The company rep told me it would be simple to use. It's easy for me, but I want feedback from someone new to the brand." She tapped the neon-blue watch that remained on her wrist. "Plus, I need to experiment with this one."

As the owner of Friend's Running, Stacey tested the clothes, gadgets, and shoes before selling or recommending them to customers. Heather considered it a perk to run with someone who got the newest gear, especially since she couldn't afford it herself. Heather fastened the watch on her wrist and fidgeted with it while Stacey and Angela threw out ideas of where Rachel could be.

"She stopped for coffee."

"She's doing her taxes."

"She deep-cleaned her carpets."

"She's paying the parking tickets she ignored so she doesn't get arrested."

"Stop! Rachel will be here." Heather's shoulders tensed. She rushed to find another excuse to stop her friends from bickering. "Maybe she's caught in traffic."

Angela and Stacey exchanged a look before Stacey said, "We live in a one-stoplight town."

"More importantly, we're making you nervous," said Angela.

Heather blurted out, "You are. Could you please stop?"

"How are you going to be a principal if you don't like a little teasing among friends?" asked Stacey. "Teenagers and their parents are going to be more vicious than this. Besides, our conversations never end in fights."

"Not true," Heather exclaimed. "Travis Gilmore, tenth grade. You both got detention for fighting about Stacey's homecoming corsage and didn't talk to each other until Spring Fling."

"That doesn't count."

"Why not?"

"You want to answer that one?" Angela asked Stacey, who scanned the cars in the parking lot.

"What?"

"Travis Gilmore?"

"Heather, give it a rest. Angela and I were sixteen. Nothing counts at sixteen."

"I concur. You aren't legally able to enter a binding contract until the age of eighteen, so anything before that is expunged from the record." Angela wrapped her arms around Stacey and hugged her. "We never stopped speaking or arguing. It's who we are."

"Travis did that on purpose. Who buys a cactus for a corsage? Stupidest thing ever."

Heather relaxed. "Technically, it was a succulent. He thought he was being sweet, since you could plant it after the dance."

"Whatever." Stacey threw her hands in the air when she saw Rachel, the fourth and final member of their running group, heading their way. "About time! You're welcome to call if you're going to be late. I know you have a phone."

"We said nine-*ish*. It's nine-ish." Rachel tucked a few strands of her glossy black hair into her hot-pink ball cap. "I'm ready. What are we waiting for?"

"Stretch," commanded Angela. "There will be no whining about pulled muscles because you ran cold."

Rachel waved away the suggestion. "As the baby in the group—"

Angela interrupted, "By a month."

Rachel ignored Angela. "As the baby in the group, I'm still resilient and don't need to stretch."

"Everyone needs to stretch," Stacey said. "We have a class on it at the store. Maybe you need to try it."

"Or search for a video online. That works for me," said Angela.

Stacey's right foot tapped the ground, signaling her impatience.

Eager to keep the calm among her friends, Heather said, "Let's get started. I need to prep to meet the school board."

Without waiting for a response, Heather took off at a slow jog down the sidewalk. It didn't take long before her friends' footfalls reached her ears and Stacey dashed past her, taking the lead as the group started its warmup.

Silence reigned for the first five minutes of their run. Heather didn't remember who set the rule or why it existed, but they never talked at the beginning of their runs. She liked to think it was to let in the sounds of nature after being stuck inside working. Maybe it was a way to let go of the stress and tension from whatever drama found them. Or it could be they needed to save their breath. Whatever the reason, the four friends continued the time-honored tradition.

Like clockwork, as soon as Stacey's watch beeped the five-minute mark, Rachel turned to Heather. "How's the next principal of Stadium High School?"

"She pulled out the running man earlier, so I'd say nine out of ten," Stacey said as she jumped over a puddle.

Rachel ran through the middle of the water, sending water splashing. Heather veered to the side before anything hit her, but the water splattered Angela's legs.

"If we needed anymore proof that Rachel is a baby, exhibit A," said Angela, shaking off her legs. "How did you not see that puddle? My shoes and socks are soaked."

Heather ignored Angela's complaints and answered Rachel's question. "Excited! I narrowed down the list of changes I want to make."

Stacey nodded in approval. "You only have so much time. Focus on one or two."

"You think four's too many? I've got plans for each of them."

"Tell us what you settled on," Angela said as she moved as far from Rachel as she could. "We know you and what you're capable of. If it's too much, we'll tell you."

"Promote mental health, add more non-sports-related clubs, allocate money for teacher room prep, and encourage technical certificates and associate degrees as much as a four-year college education." She scrunched up her nose. "That sounds like a lot when I say it out loud. Too many?"

"Yes!"

"No!"

"Maybe!"

The disagreement worried her. If the people who loved her didn't think she was on the right track, what would the school board say? The previous principal's abrupt resignation had baffled the board, and Heather wasn't their first pick as a replacement—more like the logical one. Her time as vice principal had taught her everything she needed to know, and she knew being in charge wasn't her thing. But the opportunity had come at the right time. The bigger salary would come in handy to help with her daughter's college tuition, and the principal could make some much-needed changes.

"If you set goals like those, you will burn yourself out making them happen," Angela said. "Plus, this town is all about sports. There are no sports opportunities at junior colleges and tech schools. Make the board and boosters happy. After you prove your abilities, *then* ramp it up."

Stacey waved away Angela's concerns. "I say go for it. The school needs what you have to offer. Go big or go home!"

Heather turned to Rachel. "What does 'maybe' mean?"

"It's a lot. Whittaker's supporters will not make this easy for you. People are mad at the way he left. Doesn't make sense. You've got teacher opposition, too—bumping you from vice principal to principal." Rachel shot Heather a sympathetic smile. "But if anyone can do it, it's you."

The group approached a hill, and Heather focused on her breath rather than the conversation. She inhaled through her nose, exhaling out her mouth as she leaned into the hill and shortened her stride. Running with her friends was something she could control. This new job? She didn't know.

By the time they made it to the summit, Heather gulped for air.

"Don't stop," Stacey encouraged. "Keep going."

The women kept up the pace in silence, Stacey and Angela running slightly in front of Rachel and Heather. Heather frowned when she realized that was the way they lived their lives as well. Stacey and Angela attained financial and career success where she and Rachel struggled to make ends meet.

After they'd caught their breath, Stacey called over her shoulder, "How are things with hubby?"

"The usual. Complete disagreement. On anything. He wants me to work at the dry cleaner. I made it work before, but I don't think I can keep it up this year," Heather said breathily, jealous of her friend's ability to carry on a conversation. She drew in a deep breath before she added, "Sleeping in the same room doesn't help matters. As soon as Justine heads back to college and we get back to separate bedrooms, things should get better."

"You should tell Justine what's going on with the two of you. She can handle it," Angela said. "You underestimate her."

Heather rolled her shoulders back. She'd given up on the idea of "happily ever after" years ago, when it was more important to help their daughter deal with her depression and anxiety than it was to schedule date nights. Heather didn't have the time or energy to be the perfect wife for Matthew. At the time, Heather had assumed that's what parents did for their children, and things would sort themselves out when Justine got older.

She hadn't considered the long-term effect it would have on their marriage.

But now wasn't the time to worry about that. She had other things to focus on. Like her new job.

"At least he's still there. He could have bailed. A lot of men do," said Rachel.

Guilt washed over Heather when she thought of Rachel's divorce. Heather said, "I'm sorry. I shouldn't complain."

"Just saying there is still something good coming out of the situation," Rachel said.

"He's alive, too," said Stacey. "I've adjusted to being a widow, but I'd hate for anyone else to join the club."

"Wow. This got dark all of a sudden," Angela said. "Rather than adding my thoughts about being a single professional woman in her early fifties, living in a small town where there are no eligible men, has anyone seen any good movies lately?"

The friends finished the five-mile run while debating the best and worst rom-coms of the year. Heather chimed in occasionally, but her ungratefulness weighed her down. Life hadn't given her what she wanted, but she still had more than some people. By the time they got back to their cars, Heather promised herself she would no longer complain about Matthew to her friends. Her life was fine the way it was.

Heather squirmed when Stacey headed toward her with a bright-pink gift bag stuffed with teal polka-dotted tissue paper.

"I know we're on for a celebratory drink at Lew's after you sign your contract, but we got you something." Stacey held out the bag. "It's from the three of us."

Heather pasted a smile on her face, hoping to hide her discomfort. "You didn't have to get me anything. You're already loaning me clothes."

"Speaking of which, here's the dress, shoes, and a handbag for your big day." Angela held out a garment bag and a small tote. "You will feel better because you will look amazing. Not that you don't always look good, but tomorrow is a big day."

Rachel's eyes gleamed. "This is something you can keep in your office in case you forget who you are."

"Don't give it away," Stacey said as she elbowed Rachel.

Heather peeked into the cheerful bag and forgot her embarrassment. Nestled in the tissue paper was a white resin chicken statue. Its oversized eyes bulged out from under the bright red comb on its head, and a large yellow name tag attached to its chest announced Mrs. Ramsey, Principal.

"This is amazing! I can't wait to put it on my desk!"

"We thought you needed another addition to your collection," Angela said. "This one doesn't make noise, which is even better."

"Queenie will be offended." The alpha hen in Heather's flock was louder than most hens, but she ignored her friend's comment. "Thank you all for this."

They exchanged a round of hugs, and Heather couldn't keep the smile off her face on the drive home. She may not have everything she wanted, but she had her friends. That made all the difference in the world.

CHAPTER 2

Heather danced into the house with the bags of borrowed clothes, shoes, and her new chicken. She had expected the clothes, but the surprise of the gift delighted her. The nameplate made it real—she would be the new principal of Stadium High School.

With her hands full, Heather headed straight to the bedroom to put away the gifts. She was halfway down the hall when Matthew called out, "Can you come here? I want you to look at this past-due notice."

Heather closed her eyes and let out a sigh. A few more steps and she would have avoided an interrogation about why she had so many bags if all she had been doing was meeting her friends for a run.

"I need to put some things away. Give me a minute."

Before she made it down the hall, Matthew poked his head through the doorway. His eyes widened and his eyebrows shot up.

"How did you pay for all that? We maxed out the credit cards last month."

"The girls let me borrow an outfit from their closets. No

shopping required." She took a step toward the hallway to their bedroom. "I need a shower. We ran five miles, and it was hot."

"This won't take long." Matthew disappeared into the kitchen.

She considered ignoring him. But Dr. Austen, their marriage counselor, had encouraged her to engage with Matthew when he reached out, which wasn't often. Heather hated to waste the advice, especially since she couldn't afford any more sessions. She stuffed down her irritation and followed her husband into the kitchen. A stack of papers on the table immediately caught her attention.

Her husband grabbed one paper and held it out to her. Matthew asked, "Do you recognize this?"

Heather put down her bags and took the paper. Before she could review it, Matthew asked, "Why aren't you wearing the golf shirt with the dry cleaner's logo tomorrow? It's good advertising, and that's what you wear to school with capris."

Heather stiffened. Dr. Austen had pointed out that clothing was more about function for Matthew than it was for her, which explained his question. But it grated on her nerves. Why should she justify why she wanted to look nice for her big day?

"It makes me feel good. I'll still wear the logo apparel during the school year."

She raised the paper to see what it was, but she caught Matthew zeroing in on the pink gift bag. Dropping her arms to her sides, she steeled herself for whatever came next.

"What did the girls get you this time?" Matthew walked to the counter and pulled the chicken from the bag. His expression resembled the time she'd accidentally machine-washed his bowling shirt instead of sending it to the dry cleaners. His response was the same, too. "What the hell?"

He read the words aloud before turning it toward her. The bold sans serif proclaiming Mrs. Ramsey, Principal made her smile again.

"The girls gave it to me after our run. It's for my desk."

"It's unprofessional." He placed the statue next to the bag and tissue paper. "And the contract isn't signed yet."

Heather smoothed the tissue paper before sliding it into the bag. "I sign tomorrow. What difference does it make?"

"Aren't you the one who always says, 'Don't count your chickens before they're hatched'?"

"Some of the eggs hatched? How did that happen without a rooster?" Justine asked, bounding into the kitchen, her long brown hair flying everywhere. Her eyes lit up when she saw the statue, and she picked it up. "Another chicken for your collection! How sweet! The aunties got you this, didn't they?"

Matthew's eyes flashed in irritation, but Heather smiled and hugged her daughter.

"They did. They're super excited for me to be the principal."

"So am I! Too bad you weren't the principal when I was in school." Justine put down the chicken and rubbed her hands together. "I've got some big news of my own to share. Ready to hear it?"

Heather leaned back on the counter as she snuck a peek at Matthew. Justine's announcements frequently caused turmoil, and Matthew's furrowed forehead showed he was thinking the same thing.

"What's up?" Heather braced herself for whatever bombshell her daughter dropped.

"I'm changing my major. Instead of secondary education, I'm switching to cybersecurity."

The kitchen fell silent, and Heather bit her lip. Everyone in the room knew change triggered Justine's anxiety and depression. Therapy and medication kept her conditions in check, but the cost was huge. With their credit cards maxed, Heather wondered what would happen if this major flopped.

She looked pointedly at Matthew, hoping he would shut it down. She didn't want to be the bad guy.

Instead, he smiled and said, "Better job security and pay. Can you work remotely?"

"Yes! From almost anywhere. My friend rented a house in California for a month so he could surf before work. It's an incredible setup. Better benefits than schools offer, too." Her face flushed a little when she turned to Heather. "Sorry, Mom, but it's the truth."

Heather couldn't help herself. Someone had to say the obvious. "Have you considered how stressful that job would be? You're in a good place right now. Why put your mental health at risk?"

Matthew snorted. "And being a teacher isn't stressful?" He turned his back on Heather and gave Justine a fist bump. "It's a great idea. I'm glad you're taking the initiative."

"It's gonna take a little longer to finish school. My education credits don't transfer, and there are a bunch of prerequisites." She pulled a paper out of her back pocket and handed it to Matthew. As he glanced down at the paper, his eyes bulged and the artery in his neck throbbed. Justine didn't seem to notice, and she continued her explanation. "It'll add two, maybe three more years to my school. But I can do work-study or get an internship so I can help pay the extra tuition."

"No," Matthew snapped. He cleared his throat and said in a calmer tone, "Your mom and I said we would pay for your undergraduate degree."

Heather snagged the paper from Matthew. She swallowed hard when she added up the additional tuition, then double-checked to be sure $42,000 was the right number. Even with her new position, they'd need to take out a loan. She didn't know if they'd be approved in their current situation. And whether anyone believed her, Heather knew there would be increased medical expenses for her daughter's mental health.

"Have you talked to your therapist?"

Justine crammed her hands into her pockets. "She said I

need to take control of my life. As long as I take my meds and stay consistent with therapy and self-care, she doesn't see a problem."

Heather wished there were other therapists who took their insurance, but the school district's medical plan left a lot to be desired. Rather than press the point, she shoved down the worry and concern that made her want to argue and forced a smile on her face. Even if this went poorly, there was nothing she could do to convince Justine or Matthew it was a bad idea.

"Okay, then. Congratulations!"

Her daughter's shoulders relaxed, and Heather knew she'd said the right thing, even if she'd regret it later.

Justine regaled them with more details for the next few minutes before heading up to her bedroom.

When Heather was sure Justine was out of earshot, she turned to Matthew. "Where are we supposed to get the money for that?"

"I don't know. What did you want me to do? Burst her bubble?" He reached for the paperwork and pushed it her way again. "Can you look at this bill now?"

Irritation overcame her, and she grabbed the bags of clothes, no longer feeling the joy they'd given her a few minutes ago. "No. I'll look later," Heather said, and stomped off to the bedroom.

CHAPTER 3

The sanctuary of the bedroom soothed Heather, and her shoulders relaxed. She walked to the closet and put away the clothes her friends had lent her. Heather admired Angela's gray dress, stroking the smooth linen with her hand, and encountered a lump in the pocket. She smiled. She knew what she would find before she reached in and pulled out a familiar ivory envelope with Angela's monogram.

Heather walked to the bedroom door and closed it before returning to the bed. She sat down and opened the envelope. A folded note written on matching stationery and several $100 bills fell into her lap. Heather's cheeks warmed as she picked up Angela's note.

Heather,

I know you hate this, but I can tell money is tight again. Use the cash however you see fit. It is college tuition time! ;)

Don't even think about paying me back. You're the

most amazing friend anyone could ask for, and Justine is the daughter I always wanted. I want to help, so let me.

The girls and I can't wait to celebrate with Principal Ramsey at Lew's tomorrow! You got this!

Love,
Ange

SHE CLUTCHED the note and cash to her chest, thankful for Justine's guardian angel. Heather could stretch a dollar, but without Angela's generosity, she would have maxed out the credit cards years ago to help Justine. Heather pulled out her nightstand drawer and removed a copy of Homer's *Odyssey*. She flipped open the book and tucked the money in the middle pages, where no one would think to look for it. She slipped the book back in the drawer.

Then she let herself cry.

The guilt of hiding money got stronger every time she did it. Early on, she'd told Matthew about the gifts, but the conversations ended in the same argument.

"Why would someone give their friend money?" Matthew always asked. "It's like she's bribing you or something."

So, she'd stopped telling him. She only used the gifts on Justine, and Heather never asked her friend for money. But it always arrived when a doctor's bill or tuition statement showed up.

She wiped her eyes, then stood up and peeled off her faded T-shirt. As she headed to the bathroom, her cell phone rang. She checked caller ID, hoping Justine wasn't already having a panic attack over her change of major. Instead, Heather's heart sank at the sight of her mother's name. RUTH. She held her finger over the green answer button, noticing how her finger shook. If she didn't answer now, her mother would keep calling. She tapped the answer button and mustered as much cheerfulness as possible.

"Hi, Mom. How are you?"

"Fine. I've only got a minute before I meet Marge for pickleball. Good luck at your meeting tomorrow. Not that you need it. But this is exciting. If only your dad were alive to see this."

Heather heard her mother's pickleball bag clatter to the floor.

"And he would be delighted to know his granddaughter is following in his footsteps."

Heather started to mention Justine's change of major but stopped. Knowing her mother, she would blame Heather for Justine's change of heart. She couldn't take any more drama today. Plus, Marge waited for no one when it came to pickleball, and Heather knew better than to disrupt her schedule.

"Yes, he would." That much was true. Her father would have enjoyed having three generations of teachers in the family. "I don't want to hold you up, Mom. I just got home from a run with the girls, and I need to shower. Matthew wants me to look at some bills, too."

As soon as the words were out of her mouth, Heather knew she said the wrong thing.

"More bills? Now what do you owe?"

"I don't know. Before he told me, Justine showed up and dropped her—" Heather cringed. If she wanted a shower soon, she should *not* tell her mother about Justine's new degree plan. She rushed into the first excuse that came to mind. "Dropped her purse. Did you know she had fourteen tubes of lipstick and lip gloss?"

"At least she tries. Maybe you could borrow some lipstick for your meeting tomorrow."

The distraction worked better than Heather planned, but she

didn't like the new topic any more than the one she was avoiding.

"My tinted lip balm is great. It's dual-purpose. Saves space."

Ruth snorted. "It's times like this when I feel I've failed as a mother. At least my granddaughter knows the importance of a strong lip, although she is old enough now to have a signature one."

Heather rubbed her face with her free hand, glad her mother couldn't see. Ruth had swatted Heather's hands more times than she could count growing up, but she ignored those lessons these days.

"At least tell me you're using the facial cleansing foam I mailed. You know not all soap is created equal."

Now that her mother was back in familiar territory, Heather headed off the conversation.

"Okay, Mom, I'm going to shower. I'll let you know when the contract has been signed."

"Wait. I had another question."

Her mother's questions could go on for days if she let them, but she played along.

"What's that?"

"When does Justine's student teaching start?"

Heather pulled at a thread hanging from the strap of her sagging sports bra. She didn't want to lie to her mother. But Justine could change her mind again. Nothing was ever set in stone for Justine. Heather might as well wait to make sure the change stuck before causing a ruckus with her mother.

"Second semester of her senior year."

"I knew it. Marge said it was first semester, but she doesn't know what she's talking about." Heather thought she was off the hook until her mother continued, "But Marge's knees are shot, and that's because she ran into her fifties. You're too old to be doing such a strenuous activity, dear. You only get one set of joints, and you shouldn't waste your health doing something that is going to harm you in the long run. Now, if you want to do something healthy and fun, pickleball is the thing. Great cardiovascular exercise, good for your coordination, easy on the joints, and a wonderful social event. If you'd do that, you'd meet so many more people that you wouldn't have to hang onto your friends from high school."

"I like my friends." *My friends are supportive.* She thought of the cash in her nightstand. *My friends might be the only people who get me.*

Her mother's long sigh drained the rest of Heather's energy, and Heather slid down the cabinet as her mother continued.

"Well, I wanted to say I hope it all goes well tomorrow. It's about time. If you'd done what we told you to do, then you would have been principal years ago."

And she would have been a miserable person because, instead of working with the students she adored, she would have been dealing with the drudgery of administrative tasks. But that wasn't what her mother wanted to hear.

"That changes tomorrow, Mom. Do you have anything else, or was that it?'

"There's no need to be snippy. I'm only concerned about your well-being. Someone needs to be."

Because Matthew isn't. Heather filled in what her mother didn't say. She had to admit her parents might have been right on that one, but Heather didn't have the energy or interest to discuss it now. Luckily, she didn't have to.

"I have to go. Marge is waiting."

Heather said, "I'll call you tomorrow after my meeting."

Her mother didn't respond. She'd already hung up.

CHAPTER 4

*H*eather smoothed down the linen dress after she got out of her car. Her friends' clothes fit perfectly for today's interview. Angela's boatneck dress hugged her body but still gave off a professional, academic vibe. Rachel's flair for the exotic found its way into the scarf knotted around her neck, softening the outfit in a way that made her friendly and approachable to students. The comfortable but fashionable footwear Stacey loaned her made her smile. Who knew sneaker-inspired pumps, with their supportive insoles and surprisingly comfortable two-inch heels, would complete the outfit?

She felt better today than she had in a long time. She needed as much confidence as possible. Today was a big day.

Determined and confident, Heather strode toward the district offices. Her meeting would be held in the Executive Conference Room, a location Heather had never had a reason to enter. The Board of Education reserved it for official business. She hadn't been involved in anything so serious that it needed to be dealt with in an official capacity.

She pulled open the heavy, imposing door to the building,

and a burst of frigid air hit her. Heather reached into Stacey's sable-brown leather handbag and pulled out Angela's matching sweater. She was glad she had relented when her friends suggested bringing both the purse and the coat. The bottomless pit of a purse that reminded Heather of carry-on luggage held not only the coat but also the legal pad with Angela's questions, a bottle of sparkling water Stacey said would make her look more administrative, and enough spare pens for the entire board. Just in case.

"My! I ain't seen you that spiffy since your weddin' day!" Regina, the Board of Education's administrative assistant, beamed at Heather from behind the reception desk. "Makes sense, though. Your daddy would be so proud."

Heather approached the desk, nervous about Regina's reaction. The assistant didn't give out compliments, so this was a day to remember. Heather wondered if she'd gone overboard. Maybe she should have worn the capris.

"Thanks, Regina. I'm excited about it. So excited that I let the girls dress me for the occasion."

Regina threw back her head and laughed. "Those are the friends to have. You look great. You'll knock 'em dead." She checked the monitor in front of her. "They're running a little late. A change to the agenda to fit in some new hire for the high school. The woman's from Dallas." She closed her eyes and shivered as if the city were some sort of virus. "Chairs in the hall are comfy, and someone'll call ya when they're ready. Congratulations, Principal."

Heather put her hand on the desk. "I didn't know we hired someone from the city. Do you know what position?"

Regina rolled her eyes. "Don't know, but the woman sauntered in like she owned the place. Polite but not real friendly, if you know what I mean."

Heather knew exactly what Regina meant. Stadium locals eyed anyone new with suspicion, especially if they were from a big city like Dallas or Houston. As far as most locals were concerned, city folk could stay in the city.

She waved goodbye to Regina and headed down the hallway toward the conference room. She'd worry about the new person later. As principal, it would fall on her to assimilate an outsider, and that might be difficult. The sooner the Dallas woman knew how to fit in, the better.

The shiny tile floors caught her attention, and she wondered how long it had taken to buff them to a high gloss. Maybe she'd ask the maintenance department to teach the high school's cleaning staff. It would be nice to get rid of the black scuff marks and sticky residue in the hallways, at least for a while.

Turning the corner, Heather slowed down to take in her surroundings. A sitting room with large, comfortable chairs was staged outside of the Executive Conference Room, making it look more like a high-tech business than the administrative offices for a small-town school district. There was even a crystal chandelier hanging over the seating area.

Heather snorted. Parents complained about inappropriate use of funds. She wondered what they would think if they could see this.

Settling herself into one of the oversized chairs, Heather took a deep breath. She loved being the vice principal. Interacting with the students filled her heart and soul. But becoming principal would ease the financial pressure in her life, not to mention make her mother happy. She relaxed into the chair as she imagined the freedom of no debt looming over her. No late payment notices or collection calls.

The mahogany door of the conference room swung open, and Heather looked up with a smile on her face. Mr. Hall, the school board president, stepped out, his attention toward someone behind him. Heather gathered her things and stood up as she heard him say, "It was a pleasure to meet you in person.

You'll be a great addition to the high school administrative staff."

Heather arched her eyebrows. Something told her this was the vice principal replacement and the new hire from Dallas. Her shoulders threatened to slump, but she forced herself to sit up straight. She had wanted to be included in the interview process, and she wanted to hire from within the district. There were plenty of outstanding candidates.

She reminded herself she had plenty of other things to keep her busy. The board was only trying to help. It was better to not get upset right before her first big meeting as the principal. Heather settled a neutral expression on her face and stood up, waiting for Mr. Hall to see her. Might as well get the introduction done sooner than later.

Heather scrutinized the woman emerging from the conference room. Her sleek navy-blue suit made Heather glad she'd taken her friends' wardrobe advice. The woman looked like something out of a fashion magazine. The Wedding Barn in Glen Valley had a decent suit selection, despite its name, but it couldn't compete with all the boutiques and department stores Dallas offered.

"Mrs. Ramsey. Oh yes . . ."

Heather heard surprise in Mr. Hall's voice, which was echoed in the look that darted between her and the woman in the blue suit. He hesitated, as if he had a complicated decision to make. Before he could continue, the woman reached out her hand toward Heather and smiled.

"It's nice to meet you, Mrs. Ramsey. I've heard a lot about you."

Heather shook the outstretched hand. It was cool, as if the woman weren't the least bit nervous to be starting a new job. It was also firm and confident.

"A pleasure to meet you, Missus . . . ?" Heather looked at Mr. Hall for an introduction. His gaze didn't meet hers. She frowned and looked back at the woman in front of her, whose expression morphed into that of someone who had stepped in a puddle of mud and didn't know what to do.

"Actually, it's 'miz.' I'm Shannon Parker." The woman paused, as if waiting for Heather to recognize the name. Heather gave a shake of her head. Ms. Parker glanced at Mr. Hall, who seemed otherwise occupied by the floor. Her jaw tightened before she cleared her throat. "I look forward to working with you. I'm the new principal here at Stadium High School."

CHAPTER 5

Heather froze. The woman in front of her claimed she was the new principal. That couldn't be right, because Heather had been told *she* was the new principal. She stared at Mr. Hall, who had looked up from the floor but fidgeted at her gaze. He would set this woman straight, wouldn't he?

When no one spoke, Heather clarified things for herself. "Did you say principal?"

Shannon's shoulders twitched as she nodded. "I won't keep you, but make an appointment to meet with me. We should get to know one another. It was a pleasure to meet my vice principal."

The woman turned on her three-inch heels and made her way down the hallway, leaving Heather to stare at her wake.

When Shannon disappeared around the corner, Heather whirled back toward Mr. Hall, who pointed at the conference room door.

"Mrs. Ramsey, if you could join the rest of the board inside, we will bring you up to speed."

Heather looked down the empty hallway. This outsider had

saved Heather from a role she didn't want but sank her financial life raft. She trudged through the mahogany door of the Executive Conference Room and cringed when it closed behind her. This should have been an exciting meeting, but all Heather could hear were Shannon's words echoing in her head: *"It's a pleasure to meet my vice principal."*

My vice principal.

Heather gripped the strap of Stacey's handbag with shaking hands as a wave of dizziness threatened to overpower her. She focused on taking regular, shallow breaths and forced herself to assess her surroundings.

A dark mahogany table surrounded by twelve chairs dominated the space. Two matching sideboards anchored either end of the rectangular room. A silver tea set rested on one sideboard, which Heather had read were gifts from the railroad that stopped in Stadium years before.

When the contents of the room didn't help, she turned her attention to the people. She knew them all, some better than others. What she didn't know was why several of them gazed at her like she was fresh roadkill in the middle of a highway.

"Mrs. Ramsey, please take a seat. We need to go over your contract for next year."

Mr. Hall's voice pulled her out of her brooding. Her eyes flicked over him, and she registered that his voice was no longer comforting in its authority.

"As you now know, your contract has changed slightly."

"Slightly?" Heather winced at the shrill tone of her voice and bit her lower lip. She didn't want to let on how upset she felt. She cleared her throat. "The contract is for an entirely different position."

Heather waited for someone to explain what was going on, but when no one spoke, she turned to Mr. Hall.

"Fine. Let's go over my contract." She walked to the chair at the head of the table and pulled it out.

"Mrs. Ramsey, your seat is here." Paula Jefferson, the newest school board member, pointed to a smaller chair that sat on the long side of the table.

Heather struggled to keep her composure under the gaze of two board members who regarded her like she was a petulant child, questioning instructions. Without arguing, she took the chair and waited for the board's explanation.

It seemed the board had no intention of explaining. For the next fifteen minutes, they walked her through the contract. It was the same one she'd had for the last seven years, other than the small cost-of-living increase and the large health insurance premium increase. No one mentioned the change in the contract's position, only a recitation of facts that Heather could have given herself.

"You will need to sign the contract no later than five tomorrow afternoon if you want the position," Paula said. "Do you have questions?"

Heather raised her eyebrows. Her brain raced for words that showed the board they were wrong. Blurting out what she really wanted to say would make her look unprofessional.

"Yes. I do. What is going on? Who is Shannon Parker, and why does she think I will be her vice principal?"

Heather took in the board members' reactions. Mr. Hall gazed at the corner of the room, like he was searching for cobwebs. Paula glanced at her watch. Several others stared at the papers in front of them. One filed her nails. Only Deborah Powell, the longest-serving board member, met Heather's gaze with a sad smile.

"Mrs. Ramsey, it was the board's decision to give the principal position to Ms. Parker," Mr. Hall started. "While you have all the qualifications and experience, the concern from the rest of the board—"

"That's not an accurate statement. I had no concerns. If you recall, I said this is a ridiculous idea." Deborah shook her head. "Tell her the truth. Heather deserves that much."

The outburst brought the board to life.

Two of the board members leaned together, their murmurs loud enough for Heather to recognize her own name. Mr. Hall tapped one offender, who jerked out of the way, creating a breeze that sent the papers flying in the air. Several papers hit the woman filing her nails, and she let out a cry of irritation.

"Enough." Paula banged the table with her fist to get everyone's attention. "The board does not need to explain itself to anyone, particularly an employee of the district. We provide our students a safe environment in which to learn, someplace that nurtures students so they can succeed after graduation."

"That's the school's mission—put the kids first and help them make something of themselves. You told me I was the person best positioned to do this. What changed?" Desperation sounded in her voice, but Heather had the right to know why an outsider would get the job that had been promised to her.

Paula leaned forward, both her hands on the table in front of her. "Mrs. Ramsey, we don't have to provide feedback to job applicants."

Heather blinked back her surprise. "Says who?"

"Our legal counsel."

The words felt like a bucket of ice water had been thrown over her head. She was no longer a valued member of the staff. She was a mere job applicant. Heather shuddered as she took in the rest of the faces watching her before she opened her mouth to speak.

Deborah mouthed, *"Not here,"* before she looked down at her stack of papers.

Realizing there was no more information she would get, Heather picked up her contract and stood up. "I'll have my attorney look this over and get back to you tomorrow."

"Like you said, it's the same contract you've had for seven

years." The scowl on Paula's face caught her off guard. "What's there to review?"

Refusing to be bullied, Heather walked to the door. She expected someone from the board to call out a goodbye or apologize for the events of the meeting. But when she turned back, everyone focused on the table in front of them.

Heather left the Executive Conference Room, closing the door behind her with more force than necessary. She shuffled down the hall as fast as she could, sucking in air to hold back the sobs that threatened.

Her friends had been there through the tough times she'd had with Matthew and Justine, and they were the ones she could turn to now.

CHAPTER 6

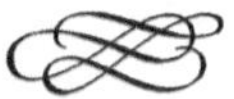

"Can someone please move these balloons?"

Heather batted the red-and-yellow mylar balloons proclaiming Congratulations! away from her face. Her friends couldn't have known how her meeting with the school board would go, but the decorations only added to her humiliation.

"I'll ask the hostess to repurpose them." Stacey grabbed the balloon arrangement from the high-top table.

"Flag down our server too? I need another drink!"

Stacey waved her hand in acknowledgment, then strode to the front of the restaurant.

"Don't get me wrong. It's been a bad day," Rachel said, "but do you really think alcohol's the answer?"

"I need you sober." Angela peered up from Heather's contract she'd been reviewing. Tapping the document with her pen, the attorney said, "I have questions."

Christine shook her head. "Tequila cures everything. If she wants to drink, let her."

"Thank you."

Heather tried to smile, but her face fell when she recognized the fountain pen Angela was using. It was the one the friends had given Angela when she made partner at the law firm. Angela saved it for cases she deemed demanding. Apparently, Heather's bait-and-switch contract applied.

"You have until Stacey brings the server back. But I don't know what else I can tell you; they gave the job to someone else. Someone from Dallas, for Pete's sake."

Rachel covered Heather's hand with her own and gave it a squeeze. "Considering the circumstances, the board could have handled things better."

Heather slapped the tabletop, and the woman at the table next to them frowned. Heather ignored her. "You're right! This is not my fault. Someone should have called me—told me what was happening."

"That's what I told 'em, but no. Why listen to me?" Regina slid into Stacey's vacant seat and let out a long sigh. "You're tough to track down." She gave Christine a nod. "The rumors are true! You're back."

Christine took a chip from the basket. "Hey, Regina. I've been back a while."

Heather frowned. Her mind was fuzzy from the margarita. She didn't remember inviting the Board of Education's administrative assistant to her party. But right now, she was so upset she couldn't think straight.

Rachel slid the bowl of salsa closer to Christine before she turned to Regina. "I've never seen you here before."

Regina helped herself to a handful of chips. "Don't usually go out, but I'm so mad I could spit." A chip flew out of her mouth and landed on the edge of the table. "The school board's outta its mind!"

Rachel slid back her chair, out of range of anymore airborne chips.

"Yeah. Heather's drowning her sorrows. This was supposed to be a celebratory evening, but we're in commiseration mode right now." Christine pulled Heather's arm out of the way as

Regina grabbed more chips. "Does the school board know you're here?" she said to Regina.

"Deb sent me. She wants you to know what happened. The rest of the board can suck it, though. Buncha idiots, if you ask me."

The server returned to the table with the tray of drinks, Stacey following. She did a double take at Regina sitting in her chair, but the assistant didn't notice. Regina pointed at the margaritas and caught the server's eye. "Can I have one o' those? It's been a tough day. Sugar, not salt, though. Gotta watch my pressure."

The server nodded without comment and headed back to the bar.

The table remained silent. Heather didn't know if it was the numbing effect of the alcohol or Regina's sudden appearance. Either way, everyone at the table seemed uncomfortable, particularly Stacey, who stood as she sipped her drink.

"I'm not gonna be here long." Regina grabbed another handful of chips, causing everyone to push their chairs back. She shoved a chip into her mouth. "But Heather deserves betta. That Paula woman talked the resta the board into hirin' an outsider. It'll haunt her, but the rest of 'em agreed. 'Cept for Deb. She stood up for ya."

Angela tentatively leaned in, although she looked ready to dodge any loose tortilla chip crumbs if necessary. "Do you know why?"

Regina's head bobbed, but when she opened her mouth to respond, she choked on a chip. She sputtered and coughed before Christine shoved a margarita glass at her. Despite the salt-rimmed edge, Regina downed it in one long gulp.

"My, my. That was good." She slid the glass back to Christine before wiping her mouth with the back of her hand. "Board doesn't wanna get burned again."

When Regina went in for more chips, Angela pulled the bowl away. "What do you mean?"

"A principal resigning out of the blue ain't normal. It's embarrassin'. Board's not gonna let it happen again. Paula convinced 'em to bring in someone from outside who's more professional." Regina rolled her eyes. "You ask me, an outsider can be jus' as squirrelly. Maybe more so. Especially when they don't know the town or its people. This Ms. Parker woman ain't gonna fit in the way they thought she would. No sir. She's got some ideas that are gonna be a problem."

"But why not tell me?" Heather heard the desperation in her voice. "Today was a train wreck."

"They owed ya that, for sure. Coulda knocked me over with a feather when Deb came outta the meetin' and told me what happened." Regina scanned the room like she was looking for spies. "You didn't hear this from me, but Deb said the board tried to get her to take the vice principal spot. She didn't like that cuz she's some award-winnin' admin from the big city. Once Paula heard that, it was a slam dunk. No award-winnin' admin is gonna leave last minute. At least, that's what the board thinks."

Tapping her fountain pen, Angela nodded. "The board caught flack for Whittaker's resignation. Makes sense that they wouldn't want to deal with that again."

"I won't resign." Heather slurred the words louder than she'd expected. "The board doesn't think I have what it takes. I was convenient. And now I'm stuck working for someone else and didn't even get a raise."

"If it's any comfort, the board thinks ya do a good job in the vice principal position. Deb went on about keepin' admin consistent, and you're nothin' but." Regina patted Heather on the back and slid out of the chair. "Which is why she wanted me to find ya and tell ya what's what. The board ain't lookin' out for anyone but itself. This ain't personal, sweetie. They're just coverin' themselves."

"Thanks, Regina, for stopping by," Rachel said. "We appreciate it."

The assistant gave a quick wave and headed away from the table as fast as she'd arrived.

Stacey plunked down on her vacant seat. "How do we feel about that information? Ange, does it matter?"

"Circumstantial. Could be premeditated, as they knew what they were doing. However, Heather signed no contract, and nobody offered anything directly."

"Bull crap," Christine said.

The woman at the table next to them cleared her throat again, but Christine glared at her. Whatever the woman wanted to say, she kept it to herself.

Christine continued, "She's been prepping all summer under the assumption of a new title and pay for the next year. They owe her something, don't they?"

Angela shook her head as she pushed the papers back to Heather.

"There is nothing in this contract or her previous one that gives her protection for what she's experiencing. The board is following the process exactly. Unfortunately, there isn't anything I can do to help. You could ask for compensation for the extra work you did to prepare for the new role, but they don't have to give you that either."

The server showed up with Regina's sugar-rimmed margarita at that moment. Heather grabbed it before anyone could stop her and slurped it down. It was a mistake, but she'd deal with it in the morning.

CHAPTER 7

*H*eather propped her elbows on the counter at the dry cleaners and cradled her forehead in her hands. The steady pounding in her head sounded like a jackhammer pounding on cement, thanks to that third margarita. She knew better. Now, on top of the fact that she hadn't gotten the principal job, she had a raging hangover.

The chime on the front door rang, and Heather squeezed her eyes shut as a starburst of fresh pain ricocheted through her head. She swallowed the bile that crept up her throat and prayed that whoever had arrived wasn't interested in talking.

Heather forced open an eye to find Mrs. Hunsinger standing in front of her. Stifling a groan, Heather cursed her luck. It had to be the woman who considered gossip an Olympic sport.

"Looks like someone partied hard last night." Mrs. Hunsinger placed a laundry bag on the counter and slid it across. "Bloody Mary will fix you right up."

Heather's stomach clenched at the suggestion. She shook her head, which made the pounding worse.

"Good morning, Mrs. Hunsinger," Heather said in a scratchy voice. The last thing she wanted to talk about was alcohol.

Mrs. Hunsinger took mercy on her and turned her attention to the laundry bag. "Cleaned out some closets and found a batch of tablecloths I'd forgotten about. Thought I'd give 'em to the church, but they need laundering first. Too big to put in my washing machine or hang up on the line. I thought Matthew could clean 'em up nice and neat for me."

Heather nodded, then stilled as the movement sent another wave of nausea through her. As smoothly as possible, she pulled the items out of the bag, tagged them, and entered them into the computer. Even the sound of her fingers on the keyboard worsened her headache.

"Have you taken any aspirin, child?" Mrs. Hunsinger asked. She reached into her brown handbag and rummaged through its contents. "I've got some in here from when Mr. Hunsinger did his rabble-rousin'. Might be expired. It's been a few years since he passed, God bless his soul."

The chime on the front door rang again before Heather could decline Mrs. Hunsinger's offer. Besides the fact that she'd taken pain killers that morning, Heather refused to consume anything out of that bag.

Both women looked over, and Mrs. Hunsinger's squeal of delight caused Heather to scrunch up her face in pain.

"Mrs. Hunsinger. Heather." Brian Glover, Stadium High School's head football coach and local celebrity, beamed at them. He held out a to-go coffee cup to Heather. "There's a rumor that you need a little pick-me-up this mornin', Sugar."

She smiled, despite her pounding head. Without tasting it, she knew it would be a perfectly made macchiato with two shots of espresso and loads of caramel sauce drizzled on top. Brian always knew what she needed. He had acquired the skill in junior high and honed it in high school while they were dating. As usual, she wondered what would have happened if they'd dated during college. But they hadn't. She'd met Matthew, and the rest was history.

Heather pulled the receipt off the printer and handed it to Mrs. Hunsinger before she accepted the sweet, caffeinated concoction and sipped. The sugar and caffeine hit her system immediately, and she moaned. "Thank you. This is what I needed."

"Bloody Mary's better if you ask me." Mrs. Hunsinger shook her head before cornering Brian. "Coach, what's your prediction for this year? We gonna win it all again? You've got the skills on the field."

Brian propped his hip against the counter and crossed his arms. Last year's state championship ring stood out against his black shirt sleeve. "Well, now, Mrs. Hunsinger, I don't want to say anything I'll regret, but the outlook is good. Practices are tight, and our QB's the sharpest I've seen in the last decade or so."

Mrs. Hunsinger winked as she tucked her receipt into her purse. "Good to know. I bought me some seats on the fifty-yard line, and I bet Willa Turner my award-winnin' cranberry salad recipe. Make sure my recipe stays in the family."

She turned for the door, but Brian beat her to it. He opened it, and Mrs. Hunsinger blushed like a schoolgirl. As she shuffled out the door, she smiled over her shoulder. "Better tell that one to lay off the tequila. Hangovers ain't for the faint o' heart."

The door closed, and Brian turned to Heather, his baby-blue eyes brimming with sympathy.

"How're you doing? Between the new principal and the tequila, I'm guessing not well."

Heather bundled the tablecloths and put them in a rolling bin. "Who told you?"

"School board president sent a welcome back email. Included a link to the new gal's bio. She did some good stuff at her old school. Not that you haven't done better things."

She took another drink of her coffee to gather her thoughts. The message was probably in her inbox, but between the gathering last night and her current state, she hadn't bothered to check.

"Lovely. Now everyone knows the board picked someone else. Was the fact that I overindulged on margaritas last night in the email, too?"

"No. That's courtesy of the Stadium gossip brigade. When I picked up the coffee, it was common knowledge you had three last night—two with salt and one with sugar. Although I hear the one with sugar was supposed to be for Regina. Lots of speculation why she'd be there with the 'runarounds.' That's not standard Regina protocol."

Heather cringed at her running group's nickname. It had been funny thirty years ago but now not so much. Neither was knowing the gossip brigade was talking about her. That was part of the joy of living in Stadium, though.

Brian flicked a piece of lint off his designer jeans. "Can Angela do anything?"

Heather put down the coffee and propped her chin in her hands. "The board verbally promised me the job, but I had nothing in writing."

He reached out, his diamond-studded wristwatch flashing in the light, and gave her shoulder a squeeze. Heather stood still long enough to accept and appreciate the gesture but stepped to the other side of the cash register. She didn't know when Matthew might appear. Her husband put up with the fact she and Brian were still friends, but in her current state, she had no desire to deal with a Matthew/Brian confrontation this morning.

Brian arched an eyebrow but didn't comment on her change of location. "You would have been a better principal. They'll regret their choice. But you're a great vice principal too. Speaking of which—"

Squeaking wheels announced the laundry cart that crashed into the front room, cutting off whatever Brian had been about to say. Heather said a silent prayer of thanks that she'd moved when she did, especially when she saw Matthew's pursed lips and red cheeks as he manhandled the cart into its position next to the register.

Matthew lifted his chin in the ritual male greeting that Heather regularly witnessed in the high school hallways.

Brian did the same and jumped off the counter before he said, "Better head out. Practice waits for no one."

"Did you have something to drop off?" Matthew asked, as if baiting the hook for an argument.

Heather tensed, hoping Mrs. Hunsinger was long gone. If the men got into it, the Stadium gossip brigade would have fodder for days.

The coach must have read her mind, because Brian put his hand on the front door before he shook his head and said, "Wanted to make sure you're still up for washing the teams' uniforms. Drop off on Saturday and return on Monday. This year it will be varsity and JV, plus the freshman team. You got bandwidth for that?"

Heather frowned. Matthew didn't have enough staff to finish his current workload, let alone two more teams, even if the money was good. Her own time in the store would be reduced once the school year started. She looked from her husband to Brian and then back again, watching them size each other up.

"That's fine." Matthew stepped out from behind the counter and leaned against it, mimicking Brian's earlier position. "Uniforms need to be here before noon on Saturday to ensure Monday delivery."

Brian's jaw clenched. Whatever was going on between the two of them had escalated from the last time she'd seen them together. No one told Brian what to do, and Matthew couldn't afford to lose this business.

But before Heather opened her mouth to intervene, Brian nodded.

"And the days we miss the cutoff, a Tuesday return works."

Matthew's eyebrows rose after Brian's acceptance of the terms. Without another word, Matthew nodded and returned to the back room.

Heather hid her relief by sipping more coffee.

"Thanks for this," she said, raising her cup. Her stomach churned. She didn't know if it was from the coffee's sweetness, the animosity between the two men, or her hangover. "I'll see you at school."

Brian stood at the doorway as if he wanted to say something else, but his blue eyes focused on the back-room door. He gave a little shrug before he winked at her and left. He strutted to his Porsche Cayenne and slid into the driver's seat. How he afforded the car on his salary was something she never could figure out, but that was the least of her worries. If he wanted to be the only person in town driving a foreign luxury car and getting teased about it, so be it.

"He's up to something."

Heather jumped at Matthew's voice, her coffee sloshing onto her hand at the sudden movement. She grabbed for a paper towel to clean up the mess.

"You always say that. The only thing he's up to is taunting you. And giving you more business than you can handle."

Matthew snorted. "I'll be fine. But you be careful around him. No one goes out of their way like that if they aren't expecting something in return."

"He's being nice, that's all. I don't know why you always think the worst of him."

"He's bribing you with caffeine, and he could have emailed about the uniforms. This is my business, and he looked at me like I shouldn't be here."

Although she'd had her own concerns, Matthew's comments grated on her nerves. "You were itching for a fight."

"Of course you'd see it like that."

Matthew ran his hand through his salt-and-pepper hair. It irritated her how his hair fell neatly back in waves, as if he had a stylist standing next to him and making him camera-ready. Despite their differences, she couldn't deny Matthew attractiveness.

"I don't have time for this. But don't you think it's odd he shows up immediately after he finds out the board hired someone from out of town? He didn't seem surprised."

Heather ignored her husband's concern. "He came by to see how I was doing and bring me a cup of coffee that he knew I would appreciate."

"I offered to get you coffee, and you said no."

Heather rolled her eyes. "You offered to reheat yesterday's leftovers. Major difference."

"But I offered." Matthew shoved his hands in his pockets, and his shoulders fell. "And he didn't get you coffee for no reason. Brian has an agenda, and he wouldn't be here if he didn't want something from you."

Matthew shuffled into the back room, leaving her alone in silence.

Heather slumped over the counter, exhausted from the exchange. Brian had been about to ask her something when Matthew came in. She couldn't argue with that. But Matthew overreacted to Brian. She was almost glad when the front door chimed again. The sound hurt her head, but more customers meant she didn't have to dwell on the problems with her husband.

CHAPTER 8

"I don't want to run today." The sun shone in her eyes, and Heather squinted to see her friends, who'd been waiting for her when she arrived at the park. "I'm only here to get out of the house. Matthew says all I do is mope."

"You're entitled," said Angela as she gave her arm a squeeze. "The school board did you a disservice."

Stacey shook her head as Rachel interjected, "And Justine's left for school again. Remember her freshman year? You cried every day that first month."

Heather leaned her head on her friend's shoulder, grateful for the distraction. "I went through a box of tissues a day. My nose was so red that Matthew called me Rudolph."

"While you were a little over-the-top, I'm not sure that nickname was warranted." Stacey played with some buttons on her running watch. "However, you are in luck. Today is a recovery day, so we can walk, not run. But keep moving. This won't count if we don't go fast enough. And remember, exercise releases endorphins, and endorphins—"

Heather, Angela, and Rachel sang out in unison, "Boost your mood!"

Stacey clapped. "You've been listening. Now, let's go!"

The four friends started their five minutes of silent warmup, Stacey setting a swift but manageable pace. Heather's gaze took in the dogs and their owners playing with frisbees as she brooded about her current situation.

Since her meeting with the school board, Heather hadn't felt like doing much of anything. Not even checking on her laying chickens in their coop, the "Poultry Palace," cheered her up. She'd spent the rest of the summer dreading the start of the school year and worrying how the teachers would treat her, knowing the board didn't believe in her enough to do the job.

Loud quacking interrupted Heather's musings, and she glanced up. She cringed when she recognized the woman surrounded by a gaggle of ducks.

"Glad to see you out and about, Heather!" Mrs. Hunsinger called from where she stood by the pond. The ducks waited impatiently as the woman paused from tossing breadcrumbs.

Heather's face warmed. She knew it was from embarrassment rather than physical exertion. Rather than respond, she waved back and sped up her pace.

"Don't let Hunsinger get to you," Rachel said. Heather had regaled the girls about the woman's visit to the dry cleaners the morning after Lew's. "Those margaritas were justified based on how the board treated you."

"It's mortifying. Being hungover in front of Mrs. Hunsinger was bad enough, but then she witnessed Brian save the day with a macchiato."

"Which Matthew is still complaining about, I'm sure," said Stacey as she stepped over a pile of poop lying in the middle of the sidewalk. "People who can't clean up after their animals shouldn't have pets."

Rachel stopped and bent down to examine the pile of excrement. "That's coyote poop. Unless someone domesticated one, the town's pet owners are off the hook."

"Why do you know what coyote poop looks like?" Heather asked, eager to change the subject.

"An informational essay I assigned last spring. Someone wrote about how her father could identify fifty kinds of scat. A mix of wild and domesticated animals. Once I got over the disgust factor, it was kind of interesting to hear how he did it and why."

"I couldn't stomach grading that assignment. Or completing it for that matter." Angela took Rachel's arm and pulled her toward the rest of the group. "Back to the issue at hand. I'm sorry there isn't anything I can do contract-wise."

Heather's shoulders drooped. "Thanks for looking into it."

"Doesn't make it right," Rachel said.

Angela nodded. "No, it doesn't. But there is a positive side."

"There is? All I see is that the one-percent-cost-of-living adjustment doesn't cover Justine's new degree program."

The group fell silent, which intensified the weight on her shoulders. She hated dragging her friends down, but nothing about this school year was turning out the way she'd imagined.

"Cybersecurity has a better long-term outlook," Angela said. "I know a company that's hiring interns. When Justine's ready, let me know. I'll write her a reference."

Stacey nodded. "She's welcome to come check out my network at the stores. I do what I can, but it would be nice to have another set of eyes on it. My recurring nightmare is someone hacking into my system and taking my business hostage."

"I have no connections or business, but I write a mean résumé." Then Rachel added, "I'm also excellent at moral support."

Heather stood taller as her friends rallied around her. Some of the gloom she'd felt lifted. "You're the best. Justine couldn't have a better set of aunties."

"Can we get back to the bright side of staying in the vice principal role?" Angela asked. When Heather nodded, Angela continued, "You get the fun stuff instead of the drudgery. Shannon is stuck with the bureaucracy and politics. Wait until she experiences the Stadium gossip brigade. You can sit back and enjoy working on the college essay clinic and career readiness sessions."

"That's a positive for sure," Rachel chimed in. "Did you want to make phone calls to parents about vaping, dress code violations, and who was doing what in the boys' locker room?"

The thought of not being the bearer of bad news cheered Heather. "Good point."

"Have you talked to her?" Stacey asked.

Heather groaned. "No. Just the infamous introduction and a few emails. I'll see her next week for our 'get-to-know-you' meeting. Who does something like that?"

Stacey reached for her hand and squeezed it. "Coming from someone who likes order, I see what she's trying to do. You had a rocky start. A meeting will let her explain her plans for the school. What she expects from you. It's going to be a change from Whittaker."

"He was so laid-back; it's probably for the best. New perspectives are good, aren't they?" Rachel asked.

Heather didn't know if she agreed with her friends or not, but before she could decide, Angela said, "I did a background check on her."

"Why am I not surprised?" Rachel asked as she tilted her head and gave Angela a wink.

"At least my research is more useful than knowing what coyote scat looks like."

"Touché. Point taken. Continue, oh Counselor Supreme."

"Counselor is fine." Angela quickened her pace. "Shannon excels at her work. Her previous school district has the highest ratings in the state. Test scores were excellent. They had a high rate of college acceptances with a higher-than-average rate of students who graduated from college. Lots of programs to help underprivileged students, and a huge amount of parent involvement. Her high school produced more merit scholars than in any other state west of the Mississippi. With her resume, I understand why the board hired her."

"How is that going to translate to Stadium?" Heather asked. "We have less than four hundred total in our high school program. She had at least that many in each grade."

Angela held up two fingers. "Twice that. Most classes capped out between 850 and 900, with a total number of students coming in at 3,400. The situation is completely different here, like comparing apples and oranges. Demographics, resources, funding . . ."

"Why walk away?" Heather asked, looking at Angela. It was times like this Heather appreciated Angela's meticulousness. Some people loved chocolate. Angela loved details.

"From what I pieced together, her ex-husband is a teacher at the school. He's getting remarried and has a baby on the way."

Rachel shook her head. "Dan and I didn't have kids, but I wouldn't want to run into him daily."

"It's not that. Turns out his fiancée was his student teacher. Shannon hired her."

Stacey stopped running, the rest of them jogging back to form a circle around her. "If Rachel was telling this story, I'd accuse her of making it up."

"That's not fair!" Rachel threw up her arms. "Just because I like to embellish things a bit doesn't mean I make them up. Although this story sounds fishy to me."

"I verified it with three sources. She's separating her personal and work lives," Angela said. "But it will be interesting how she explains a switch from Dallas to here. Stadium can't compare to where she's from."

"If you found this out, the gossip brigade will too," Heather pointed out.

Stacey's watch beeped. "Damn it, Ange. Your news messed up my heart rate. Enough navel-gazing. It's time to get your butts in gear."

CHAPTER 9

The get-to-know-you meeting should have been called the pile-work-on-you meeting. Shannon assigned Heather so much work that her to-do list overflowed, but Heather had to admit Shannon was organized.

Heather gazed around the principal's office. Despite how she felt about Shannon, the room welcomed and calmed her. A year-at-a-glance calendar hung on one wall, already marked with important in-service dates and district meetings. Books sat alphabetically on the shelves. A large box of hardware rested on the otherwise clear credenza. A handmade coffee mug rested next to the computer. This was a far cry from the piles of papers and crumpled paper cups Whittaker decorated his office with.

She returned her attention to Shannon as the principal said, "You'll be quarterbacking the major changes I have planned. It's best I get you in the game as soon as possible."

Heather snorted at Shannon's unintended joke, the first she'd made. But her giddiness ceased when Shannon frowned. The woman was serious. Heather faked a cough to hide her misunderstanding.

"Sorry. Allergies."

Shannon cocked her head as she perched on the corner of the desk. Heather looked down at her notepad, glad she hadn't said what popped into her head. *"All you're missing is a whistle around your neck, and you could be Coach Glover,"* would not have gone over well.

Shannon continued. "Let's discuss the new attendance plan. What's your take on the football team? Do you think the changes will affect the players?"

Heather considered this her first test of the meeting. She wanted to make sure Shannon understood what to expect from Stadium. "Yes. Most of the team members work on their family farms or ranches. They miss a week or more during busy times."

"Missed time needs to be made up, and any consequences as prescribed by the state athletic board will be enforced." Shannon tapped her sky-blue high heel on the corner of the desk and shook her head. "Am I to assume that the football team flaunted the rules last year?"

Heather sat up straighter. "*Flaunted* might be harsh. But the offensive line spent the better part of September in the fields."

"I might regret asking, but where was the defensive line?"

"In school. The defensive line consists mostly of cattle ranchers. Calving season's in spring." Heather hesitated before she added, "But the players spent more time in the gym and workout rooms than classrooms."

"Whittaker allowed this. Why?"

"Stadium High School wins football championships. It's the bread and butter of the community. Many students stay here or in the surrounding community their entire lives. This is their chance to shine." Since Shannon seemed interested in promoting education over sports, Heather offered one of her own ideas. "I had planned to emphasize trade school as much as four-year colleges. It would give the students something else to strive for, besides providing skills that are usable on or off farms or ranches."

A flutter of butterflies exploded in Heather's stomach.

Shannon nodded and said, "We can discuss that in the future, but this year, we're tackling money. The easiest way to do that is to improve attendance and cut costs. You're in charge of maximizing attendance hours. After-school makeup hours are required. Football players will be there if they miss school. They may not attend practice or participate in games until they make up their hours."

"Coach Glover will not like that," Heather said. The flutter froze, and her excitement disappeared.

"I don't care. This school—this district, for that matter—is at the bottom of the barrel. The football team shines, but these students deserve the state money allocated to them. If the parents and coaches can't see that, too bad. It's your responsibility to make sure the teachers are recording attendance correctly and adhering to the late homework policy: a zero is required for late work." Shannon raised a hand when Heather opened her mouth to protest. "It doesn't matter if it keeps the players out of the game. If they don't learn now, they'll never learn. Next. I'm putting you in charge of digital textbooks."

Heather frowned. "What digital textbooks? You said to focus on saving money, and that's not in the budget. Plus, school starts in two weeks. How would we implement a big change like that?"

Shannon turned to the credenza and opened the hardware box. She removed a digital tablet and put it in Heather's hand.

Heather examined it. It was brand-new, although not the latest version available. She looked up at the principal, who sat down in her chair and folded her hands on her desk.

"It won't be easy, but we have the resources we need. The state awarded the district a grant for digital devices a year ago. Stadium purchased the devices six months ago, but they've been in storage since they arrived. The district's current textbook contract includes e-book rights, but, again, no one used them."

Shannon paused, and Heather focused on the questions swirling in her head. *How did the district get a grant without the teachers knowing? Why would Whittaker not tell anyone about this technology?* And her biggest question was, *Can this be implemented in two weeks?*

"This is amazing. I mean, stressful and overwhelming, but amazing." Heather looked up to see Shannon smiling at her. "You think we can get this rolled out?"

"There will be hiccups and transition issues, but yes. This will be a tremendous benefit to the students and the teachers, whether or not they like it. IT has already started loading the tablets with the correct apps. The IT manager will reach out to you with the training protocol. You're in charge of distributing the tablets, too. Get me your plan by the end of today to review."

Heather blinked at the quick turnaround. Her mind raced as a list of action items popped into her head. She wasn't sure how she would manage, but she would give it her best shot. Heather stood up and gathered her stuff. "I'll get to work then."

"Hold on. We're not finished."

"There's more?" Heather seated herself and pushed back the tsunami of overwhelm that threatened to pull her under.

Shannon tapped a piece of paper on her desk. "There are a few other issues that need to be addressed. Stricter adherence to the dress code is essential. I've been told inappropriate T-shirts, ripped jeans, and hats are worn indoors. The policy hasn't changed, but it needs to be enforced."

Stadium students hurried straight from their farm or ranch chores to make it to school on time. They didn't have time to change into jeans without holes, but Heather kept her thoughts to herself and added "dress code" to her to-do list.

"Why do we have students parking in the teachers' lot?"

Heather shrugged her shoulders. "It's first come, first served."

"From now on, we have reserved spots for teachers. Revise

the staff handbook and the student handbook. Email me your changes. I'll review each of them and make comments."

Shannon paused, and Heather felt a bead of sweat drip down her back. She was fast approaching her limit on how much additional work she could take.

"The board and I feel there are some needed revisions to the athletic booster program as well. What are your recommendations on how to communicate outside of school?"

Heather clenched her jaw. This discussion was a waste of time. How could the school board hire someone who didn't know how to share information? She willed herself to relax and said, "The school has social media accounts on all the big platforms. You can use those, but if you want to reach citizens without students in school, most people follow *The Glen Valley Gazette*'s website."

When Shannon looked at her in confusion, Heather explained, "Stadium doesn't have a newspaper anymore. *The Gazette* covers several towns and counties. It's got good distribution." Heather left out *The Gazette*'s tendency toward an entertaining and creative interpretation of the facts. "Most people have a subscription, and those who don't will hear about it from the Stadium gossip brigade."

Shannon looked at Heather as if she was speaking a foreign language. "What is a gossip brigade?"

Heather paused. She didn't know how the group got its name or when it started. She'd never thought to ask. Shannon's expression told Heather that not every town had a group like this.

"It's the unofficial title for the folks who hang out around town and talk. Most of them have nothing else to do with their time. They gossip. The exact members of the group change, but right now, the main conspirators are Mrs. Hunsinger, Mrs. Taylor, and Mrs. Edwards."

"Sounds like a bunch of busybodies to me."

If she weren't so frustrated with the situation, Heather might have grinned. "I wouldn't say that to their faces. Mostly they're harmless. Think of them as social media for the technologically impaired. The brigade's ability to spread a message exceeds anything the Internet offers."

"I'll take that into consideration if I ever have a news flash. Does the Board of Education know about this brigade?"

"Mrs. Hunsinger is Paula Jefferson's mom."

"Why does that not surprise me?"

Heather cleared her throat to prevent a laugh. She said, "Be careful what you say around Paula. If you want everyone to know, that's the place to start."

"Good to know. Our new booster policy will be welcome news to the brigade."

Heather leaned forward, waiting to hear about the changes.

"It prohibits anyone who works in the district or their immediate family from making donations to the athletic department."

Heather rocked back in her seat at Shannon's words. She tried to wrap her head around the change and failed. The town ostracized anyone who didn't contribute. Stadium Dry Cleaners didn't stand a chance if they weren't eligible to join the Stadium Booster Club. What would she and Matthew do about Justine's tuition?

"The board knows about this? Every one of them is also a booster."

"Not anymore. The board approved the change. This way, no one can complain about favoritism. The booster club is for community members only."

Heather grappled with her panic. "But the school needs money. Businesses want to contribute. Most of the owners graduated from Stadium and are happy to give back." She neglected to mention the competition among local businesses as to who contributed the most. That was neither here nor there. "You're leaving money on the table."

"I ran the numbers. It isn't as much as it could be. Last item." Shannon changed the subject, making it clear there was no room for discussion. An icy shiver of trepidation ran down Heather's back. Something told her she would not like this either. "The board asked me to let you know they signed a contract with Horton's Cleaning Services to handle the school's laundry."

Heather froze. It wasn't until she felt lightheaded that she remembered to take a breath. "Wait. What?"

"Stadium Dry Cleaning no longer has the school's laundry contract."

Ice crept into Heather's veins as the image of Justine's tuition bill flashed in her head. Things were tight, but without this school contract, the dry cleaner's revenue would plummet. Bile rose in Heather's throat, and she swallowed it back before she asked, "Do you know why?"

"The board didn't say, although it signed the contract in June." Shannon studied Heather. "The fact that your husband owns Stadium Dry Cleaning is a conflict of interest. I'm not sure how you made it this long without someone complaining."

"Stadium's a small community. We look out for each other. When there's only one option, people don't worry about it."

Shannon gave a small shake of her head. "There is more than one option. Horton's is not that far away, and they were more than happy to accommodate the school. I'm sorry to point this out, but your husband has competition. He should keep that in mind."

Heather bristled. The last thing she needed was more conflict with her husband, and that's exactly what would happen if she shared the principal's warning with him. She had no intention of telling Matthew anything.

But Shannon needed to know something.

"Are they doing the football uniforms too?"

"That was part of the deal."

"The uniforms will come back pink. Everything comes back pink from Horton's."

Shannon paused, giving Heather a glimmer of hope that the situation could be salvaged, but Shannon gave a curt nod. "Noted."

After their meeting, Heather schlepped back to her office. Her stomach twisted. Her workload had tripled in the matter of a meeting, and her financial future appeared to have tanked. While the pink uniforms promised some entertainment later in the year, Heather couldn't help wondering what her husband would say when he found out.

That was a problem for later. Right now, she needed a plan to distribute four hundred tablets to students in less than two weeks and train a group of technology-phobic teachers how to use them.

CHAPTER 10

"The compliance videos are due tomorrow. You haven't even started them."

Heather peeked over her laptop to watch Rachel. She'd taken refuge in Rachel's classroom when the teachers trickled in and found the principal's door closed with a sign directing them to make an appointment. After two days of teachers coming to her, Heather needed a quiet place to work. But Rachel was making her nervous.

Rachel looked up from the textbooks she was flipping through. Every few pages, she erased something. "I watched them last year. What's changed?"

"Nothing. But they're mandatory." Heather waved at her laptop. "I'm the monitor this year. If the dashboard says you haven't watched them by Friday, you're in trouble."

Rachel closed the textbook and balanced it on the already-too-tall stack next to her desk. "What's Shannon going to do to me? School starts in less than a week, and she's short teachers. I'm safe. If me rebelling makes you uncomfortable, you can always go back to your office."

"I told you. The admin wing is crawling with people wanting

the 411 on the new principal. I thought it would be quieter here. I was wrong."

"You like hanging out with staff." Rachel raised her eyebrows as she picked up another book and flipped it open. "Why do you need quiet?"

"Shannon gave me a bunch of assignments to finish before the work sessions start tomorrow. I can't accomplish anything with all the interruptions, although I'm not making much progress here, either."

Rachel's eyes gleamed when she asked, "What are you working on? Something more interesting than Whittaker's usual?"

Biting her lower lip, Heather hesitated. Shannon hadn't sworn her to secrecy, but the principal seemed like the type who wanted to control the release of new procedures. Heather didn't want to go into tomorrow's meeting completely unaware of how teachers would react. "You can't tell anyone about this—"

"You don't have to tell me that," Rachel interrupted.

"You've been known to share things that aren't common knowledge."

Scrunching up her nose, Rachel said, "I know the difference between public and private information."

"Really? Who told the Quiz Bowl team their sponsor was dating the FFA sponsor?" Heather's stomach gurgled at the thought of the incident. "And, frankly, this has bigger consequences than Michael and Tina getting written up."

Rachel waved away the discussion. "Poor judgment on my part. Now, what is Shannon changing that is going to get everyone's panties in a ruffle?"

"Three things. Only one of them has a major panty-ruffling effect, although the other two may cause a minor kerfuffle."

Heather turned her laptop to face Rachel. Her friend glanced at the screen with a frown.

"Why am I looking at the attendance tracking program?"

"No more excused absences for farm or ranch work. And zeros for all missed or late work."

Rachel's eyes widened, and she dropped the book she was holding.

"That's bigger than a panty ruffle. I'd say it's more like a turd on a picnic blanket. What's the football team going to do?"

Heather shrugged, then stood and paced the classroom. "Lose games. I explained the situation, but since attendance is the school's biggest problem, Shannon started there."

"Does she know what she's getting into?—going up against the football team?"

Heather pulled at the hem of her shirt. "Doesn't seem to care. She's worried about state funding. We've lost a lot of money, and she thinks tightening things up will help, which is why I was christened 'attendance czar.' Every Tuesday and Thursday after school, I monitor students who need to make up attendance hours."

"Does that come with a crown and scepter, or is it title only?"

Heather closed her laptop. "Title only. Nor does it come with the usual stipend for the extra hours I'll be spending on campus."

"How's that fair?" Rachel asked. "Everyone around here gets a stipend. Why shouldn't you?"

"Shannon said it is part of the vice principal role in assisting with disciplinary measures." Rachel opened her mouth, but Heather held up her hand. "Yes, Angela checked my contract, and, yes, I am contractually obligated to comply with Shannon."

The room fell silent except for the bits of conversation that drifted in from the hallway.

"What else is she changing?" Rachel asked.

"We're moving to digital books. No more textbook checkout."

"You let me work on these anyway, knowing it didn't

matter? That's mean." Rachel leaned down to pick up a book and turned to a page decorated with lewd and phallic images. "Not that I'm going to miss this."

Heather took the book from her friend and put it back in the pile. "Neither will I, but what about the non-tech-savvy teachers? Some already struggle with the online attendance program. How are they going to teach without a book in front of them?"

"Most of them have their subjects memorized. I wouldn't worry too much about that." Then Rachel asked, "What's the third thing?"

"No more open-door policy at the principal's office. You'll have to make an appointment."

Rachel shrugged. "Seems like a nonissue."

"What about parents showing up to complain their student athlete has been benched from a game? Can you imagine Mr. Johnson making an appointment?"

Rachel threw back her head and laughed. "The unofficial king of throwing steer? No way is he going to make an appointment! That man does *what* he wants *when* he wants. Shannon does not know Stadium doesn't work like Dallas. She's in for a surprise."

"Who's in for a surprise?" Brian asked. He stood in the doorway, holding a paper plate full of cookies. When neither Heather nor Rachel answered, he walked into the room and handed the plate to Heather. "And why are you hiding out in the English department? It makes it hard to deliver treats."

Rachel's eyebrows rose at Brian's comment, but she kept her mouth shut and reorganized her desk. Heather needed to explain to her friend that making yourself busy didn't equate to making yourself invisible, but that was a conversation for later.

Heather took the plate and recognized homemade chocolate chip cookies.

"To what do I owe this pleasure? Mrs. Johnson doesn't make these until the football team wins its first game."

Brian leaned a hip onto Rachel's desk and crossed his arms.

"I asked her. You've had a tough start to the year. Thought you needed a pick-me-up."

From behind Brian's back, Rachel stuck her finger in her open mouth, pretending to gag. Heather kept a straight face, thankful that Brian couldn't see Rachel's gesture.

"You didn't answer my questions," Brian said. "Either of them."

When Rachel rolled her eyes, Heather grabbed a cookie and took a bite. She needed something to keep her from laughing. That was the thing about working with Rachel—she found humor in all the wrong places.

"Hmm," she mumbled as she chewed. "Good."

Brian's eyes narrowed before he looked over his shoulder and caught Rachel shaking her head.

"What?" he asked.

"Do I get a cookie?"

He shrugged. "They're for Heather. Ask her."

Without a word, Rachel walked around the desk, plucked two cookies off the plate, and sauntered out the door. Heather knew she would get an earful when her friend returned.

"What was that all about?" asked Brian.

Heather waved a hand as if she were shooing away a pesky gnat from her cookies. "Nothing. Everyone's a little on edge about the new principal, which is what we were talking about when you walked in. The welcome she gets from the faculty and staff might surprise her."

Brian slid up on Rachel's desk, reminding Heather of when he sat on the dry-cleaning counter. Brian made himself comfortable wherever he went. She wondered if that was why his presence consumed the room. Or made him an excellent football coach.

He nodded. "Change is tough. But she's got the state football champions. What else could she need?"

A better attendance record, thought Heather, but Brian would find that out tomorrow along with everyone else.

"Thanks for the cookies." She took another bite before asking, "How did you know to look for me here?"

Hopping off the desk, Brian said, "You're predictable, Sugar. If you aren't in your office, you're with your friends." He pulled an envelope from his back pocket and flashed her a radiant smile. "Can you take my report to the district office?"

Heather sighed as she took the envelope and waved it at him. "I'll take this one, but I'm not making regular trips anymore. Why don't you email these? Or throw them into the interoffice mail?"

"Aw, Sugar, everyone knows I don't do email. And mail gets lost. But if the vice principal delivers it, it's gonna make it." Brian winked at her and strolled out of the room.

Heather dropped into the chair and wondered how many more duties she would accumulate this year. "Attendance czar" was bad enough, but "football postmaster" was excessive. Plain old vice principal sounded pretty good.

An excited buzz filled the library as every teacher, staff member, and assistant crowded into the room for the highly anticipated kickoff meeting with the new principal. Heather observed the controlled chaos.

The English department snagged the comfy reading seats near the fiction bookshelves. The librarian slapped Rachel's feet from the worktable before rushing to the history teachers who were eating snacks where they shouldn't be. As soon as the librarian turned her back, Rachel propped her feet back up.

The math department secured a table at the back of the library, closest to the doors. Heather could see sheets of paper on the table, a sure sign the annual betting process had begun. When Whittaker was in charge, popular bets included how many times he mentioned the football team (seventy-three was the record), whether his socks would match (once in eight years), and whether he had a booger in his left nostril (Every. Single. Meeting.).

The science department claimed the table closest to her, but Heather noticed Mr. Hollis, the department head, wasn't there. Mr. Hollis had confided in her last week that he was still upset about Mr. Whittaker's resignation. He hadn't mentioned skipping the meeting, so she scanned the room for him. She didn't find him, but she caught tidbits of conversations drifting from the various hushed conversations.

"This ain't no Dallas."

"Do you think she can shape up the science department?"

"She better not switch the coffee in the break room. That Colombian blend is perfection."

"Poor Heather—watching this woman waltz in and take her place? I couldn't do it."

Heather bit her lip. She knew it was her job now to support the new principal, but hearing someone else call out the injustice made it hurt worse.

The library door opened and stopped her ruminations. Silence fell until Brian poked his head in, and a nervous twitter erupted. The coach ambled through the room, shaking hands here and there, before he took a chair at the table with the science department.

Even though he leaned forward like he was talking to Heather, his voice carried through the entire room. "Kinda odd to be late for your first meeting, isn't it?

She squirmed in her seat. Heather didn't know what Shannon's meeting etiquette was, but it was strange to cut things this close on the first official meeting of the work week. Especially when everyone else had arrived early.

"You gonna get us started, Sugar?"

Several of the teachers nodded.

"You should. Just because the new principal can't be on time, shouldn't impact us," the English department head said. "Least she could do was make a good first impression."

A few other teachers mumbled their agreement.

Other than what Shannon had assigned to her, Heather didn't know what the rest of the meeting agenda was, and she wasn't about to start something she couldn't finish. But, from the grumbles coming from the corners of the library, she needed to do something.

She stood up and addressed the faculty. "I'm sure Ms. Parker will be here shortly. In the meantime, you could use this time to discuss—"

The library door opened again, and all attention shifted. Shannon strutted in, her blue suit and beige high heels setting her apart from everyone else's jeans and tennis shoes. She glanced around, taking in the room. Heather swore she saw a flash of a grin on Shannon's face, but it was gone before she could be sure. Heather noticed Shannon's raised eyebrow as she passed Rachel, whose chair wobbled to one side in her hurry to return her feet to the floor.

"Thank you for being here on time. Let's get started." Shannon strode up the center of the room and stood next to Heather. "Mrs. Ramsey, I can handle it from here."

Heather's cheeks warmed at the not-so-subtle inference. Hoping her face wasn't as red as she imagined it was, Heather sat down and opened her laptop to take notes. She had been the unofficial secretary for Mr. Whittaker's staff meetings, so she assumed Shannon would want the same.

When the room remained silent, Heather looked up. Shannon stood pencil straight, her gaze taking in the faculty. She seemed relaxed, as if she addressed new groups of teachers regularly. She held everyone's attention, something Heather had never seen before. Usually, teachers multitasked during meetings, but not today. No one was distracted. All eyes were on the new principal.

"Good morning. Let me introduce myself. My name is Shannon Parker. You can call me Ms. Parker." She waited a few seconds for that to sink in. "My previous position was as principal of Burgess High School in Dallas. For the last decade, it was my privilege to work with the top-ranked public school in the state. Many of you are probably wondering why I'm here in Stadium High School."

She paused, and the teachers leaned forward in anticipation of the juicy tidbit of gossip that was about to be released. It reminded Heather of Sunday church services when the pastor waited for the congregation to chime in with an amen.

"I love a challenge," said Shannon, "and you have several here at Stadium."

Voices muttered throughout the room. Heather saw the principal's grin this time. It lasted three seconds before Shannon's face returned to neutral. Whatever the principal had wanted to happen, it happened.

Shannon continued, "We have a busy week ahead of us, but before we dive into meetings, I'd like to highlight some changes you will see this year. The first one many of you may have already guessed: I meet with people on an appointment basis."

A collective groan went through the crowd, and this time, when Shannon smiled, it remained on her face.

"It's not that bad. In my experience, open-door policies lead to unnecessary meetings. If an issue is worthy of a meeting, it can wait until a time that is good for all parties involved. It keeps meetings short and sweet. I've learned over the years it's best not to have an open-door policy if accountability is an issue."

Heather's jaw dropped. What was this woman talking about? The teachers at Stadium High School were responsible. Other than Mr. Whittaker's resignation, there had been no scandals or recriminations in Heather's time at the school.

One of the math teachers raised a hand, and Heather exhaled. She didn't have to follow up on Shannon's statement. He was doing it for her.

"Yes, Mister . . . ?"

"Mr. Hanson. I teach—"

"Michael Hanson. Geometry, trigonometry, and calculus. And you're the Quiz Bowl sponsor."

He hesitated, but Shannon motioned for him to continue.

"Will this appointment policy apply only to teachers and staff, or are parents going to be asked to make appointments as well?"

"Excellent question." Shannon rubbed her hands together as if she were excited to address the topic. "Parents will be required to make appointments. I expect there will be an influx of requests when the new digital textbooks and attendance policies roll out."

The room fell silent, and Heather stiffened in her chair. It reminded her of the final minute in last year's state football championship. Stadium needed a field goal to win, and you could have heard a pin drop that night as they waited for the ball to sail through the uprights.

Shannon continued as if she didn't notice the shift in the room's atmosphere. "We have instructional sessions scheduled for all major changes, but let me give you a quick summary. Students and teachers will receive tablets with the digital content preloaded. This content is the same as the curriculum you've previously used. A side benefit of using tablets is that student lockers are no longer needed. This improves the safety and security of our school. Mrs. Ramsey will distribute all tablets and digital resources."

Heather felt dizzy, and she realized she was holding her breath. She forced herself to inhale and exhale as she listened to Shannon.

"Speaking of Mrs. Ramsey, she oversees the second change I want to highlight: the attendance policy. Stadium High School will follow the state guidelines. I encourage you to review them, but the key point to remember is that all missed hours must be made up. No exceptions, regardless of the reason."

Several hands flew in the air, but Shannon shook her head. "Let's hold questions until I'm finished."

The hands dropped, but many teachers scribbled on notepads or tapped on their phones. Heather wondered if the math department had a betting pool for the most controversial item on the agenda. This one would lead the way.

"Each of you will be audited on your adherence to the attendance policy. I understand this could impact various athletic teams. While sports are important for many reasons, we are in the business of education. That is our focus. By adhering to the policy, we will receive more state funding."

"A state football championship brings in money." Brian leaned back in his chair, the front two feet off the ground, and crossed his arms. "Respectfully, Mrs. Parker, things in Stadium don't work the way they did in Dallas."

Several comments of, "That's right," and, "About time someone said it," made their way to the front of the room, and Heather cringed. Something told her now was not a good time for Brian to insert himself into the conversation.

"It's *Ms.* Parker, and you would be Coach Glover."

He dipped his head, his chin brushing against the collar of his shirt, but he did not apologize for getting her name wrong.

"Well, Coach Glover, thank you for your contribution. I hear the team is highly ranked, and I look forward to attending Friday-night games this fall."

Brian peacocked, and he settled the chair down on four feet. "You're welcome any time to come down on the sidelines and see how things are done."

His words sounded benign, but everyone understood. This was a challenge. It seemed the teachers didn't think it was a smart play, though, with all the shifting of chairs and clearing of throats.

The corner of Shannon's mouth lifted, and Heather guessed

that the principal recognized the gauntlet that was being thrown her way.

"I'll consider it. Although I get things done as well." She turned back to the room. "Which is why the attendance policy will be strictly enforced. All absences, including sickness, will be made up. Illnesses and doctor's appointments will only be excused with a doctor's note, which will go through an internal verification system that Mrs. Ramsey will oversee. Absences because of school activities," she stared down at Brian, "including football games, practices, and training, will need to be cleared by me prior to the absence. Makeup time is required."

Silence filled the air as if everybody in the room held their breath, waiting for Brian's reaction. Everyone knew he managed the football players' time during the season down to the second. Losing precious after-school time was not something he would accept.

Heather swallowed hard when the vein in Brian's forehead throbbed, a sure sign that his feathers were ruffled.

But before he could respond, Shannon turned to the group. "The floor is open for questions."

She made quick work of the questions, her answers concise, directing teachers to the informational meetings and the upcoming department sessions. Heather watched in awe, impressed at how well Shannon handled the situation, even when Brian asked, "If I take a sick day, do I put in extra hours after school?"

The stare Shannon shot him would have wilted any other staff member. "Use your PTO. But all *students* will follow the policy. Our first session starts in fifteen minutes. Everyone should take a quick break and meet back here so we can get started on time. Whatever other questions you might have, email me or bring them to our group meetings. Thank you for your time."

Heather kept her gaze on the table, but she could hear Shannon's heels click on the floor as she made her way out of the library.

No one spoke until the door of the library closed.

Then pandemonium broke out.

Heather let the complaints, whining, and discontent wash over her as she sucked in deep, calming breaths. Not getting the principal's position wasn't the worst thing that could happen to her, but she thought dealing with this frustrated pack of teachers might do her in.

CHAPTER 12

It was tough, but Heather survived the teacher workweek. She needed some decompression time before she faced Matthew, so she detoured to the Poultry Palace. Caring for her chickens calmed her. She also felt close to her dad in the Palace. It was the last building project he had completed, and it was his magnum opus.

She ran her nails across the chicken wire, and her brood clucked its way to the front of the coop.

"Hello, ladies. How was your day?" The hens pecked the floor, anticipating dinnertime. "Better than mine, I'd guess."

The late-afternoon breeze blew Heather's hair in her face, and she brushed it aside as she entered the coop and started her routine. Heather filled the feeders and stepped out of the way as the birds made their way to dinner. Queenie, the matron of the coop, had organized the brood early on, and no one, including Heather, deviated from Queenie's system. The beak scars on Heather's legs proved it. Queenie ate at the first feeder, Beatrice and Eugenie at the second, and Tarin and Lourdes perched at the third.

Satisfied the birds were comfortable, she raked out the

soiled bedding. The familiar actions quieted Heather's agitation. The chickens had an easy life. Sure, the coop confined them, but their basic needs were accounted for. They had a regular supply of food, plus mealworms, crickets, blueberries, and watermelon as treats. Being a chicken seemed like an easier option than being the wife of a business owner who was no longer the official dry cleaner of the Stadium High School Buccaneers or part of the booster club. Not that she wanted to eat insects.

Once she replaced the bedding, Heather searched for eggs. The hens tended to lay early in the morning, and Heather collected from them before she left for the workday. But as she liked to tell her students, it never hurt to double-check.

That attitude made Matthew look at her like she had two heads. He didn't understand the fact that, even if her brood didn't leave her any eggs, she still found it reassuring to spend time with them. They weren't pets, but she knew what to expect from them. Feed them. Water them. Collect the eggs. Nothing less. Nothing more.

She found one egg and took it with her as she left the enclosure. Heather locked down the coop for the night, making sure the door was secure, in case a fox or coyote came by looking for easy prey. Heather prided herself on never losing a chicken to anything but old age. She didn't want anything to change that now.

Rather than walking to the house, she sat down on the lawn chair next to the coop. She was stalling. She'd avoided Matthew all week, not wanting to be the person who told him about the changes at the school. Tonight, she didn't have the energy for the conversation. Taking deep breaths through her nose, she watched the chickens and thought about her dad.

She often wondered why he hadn't built more chicken coops. It was the one time she saw him look happy and satisfied. He had talked about being a principal and was proud of his accomplishments, but she didn't remember seeing him as proud as the day he pulled the Palace into her backyard.

The automatic timer clicked, and the overhead lighting turned off. That was one perk her dad had added to the coop. He equipped it with a chandelier made of old crystals and glass beads he'd found at yard sales and the dump. The breeze made the chandelier in the coop swing, the soft tinkling sound a soothing background for the chickens as they scratched and searched for any remaining food.

Her dad had worked with his hands to clear his head, and, while she never followed his example, she appreciated what he was doing. The calmness of the chicken coop soothed her, letting her brainstorm solutions for their current financial issues. Matthew's business couldn't sustain a big hit, like losing the school contract. They needed a break, and fast.

The easiest option was to take out loans for Justine's tuition. It would only delay the problem. But they'd finally paid off the loan from her master's program, and it was one thing she and Matthew agreed on—don't borrow more money.

She brainstormed other areas. Cable TV could go. The grocery budget could stand to be trimmed down. Speaking of trims, she made a mental note to cancel her upcoming haircut and color. Might as well take one for the team.

Queenie clucked, drawing Heather's gaze. The chickens cost money she and Matthew didn't have right now. But they produced fresh eggs and made her happy. Heather watched the girls scurry around the coop. She couldn't part with the girls. She sighed and kept thinking.

The latest envelope of cash from Angela was a stopgap. Next semester would be here in the blink of an eye, and Heather knew going without cable and a haircut wouldn't solve the problem.

A second job was an option. The timing wasn't great with

the extra work Shannon had piled on her. There wasn't much in town Heather could do outside of school hours, either. It would take time and money for gas to commute to one of the surrounding towns. Plus, that added wear and tear to her car. Her reliable Ram was trustworthy, but it had seen better days.

Letting everyone go from the dry cleaners would save money, maybe even enough to cover Justine's increased tuition. Matthew would endure that, but Heather could work Saturdays and Sundays, which was what he wanted anyway. He might even be so excited she'd finally acquiesced that he wouldn't even try to say it was his idea.

Heather smiled for the first time since she'd been home. There was a solution, and she'd found it with no one's help.

Ready to face her husband, Heather turned to the house in time to see Matthew striding through the yard toward her. She hesitated. Matthew didn't come to the chicken coop unless something was wrong.

Chastising herself for being negative, Heather pasted a smile on her face. "Haven't seen you down here for a while."

"We need to talk." He waved a sheaf of paper in his hand as he approached.

Heather twitched. "We do. I should update you on the changes at school."

The lines between Matthew's eyebrows furrowed, and he braced himself on the back of the empty lawn chair. "Let's start with the fact that Stadium Dry Cleaning has been replaced by Horton's."

Heather's jaw dropped. She struggled for words, but nothing came out of her mouth.

Matthew nodded and crossed his arms, the papers sticking out at weird angles. "Hmm. That explains Brian's visit and his perverse pleasure in delivering the news."

"He stopped at the cleaners?" Heather couldn't remember

the last time the coach had dropped by when she wasn't working. "What else did he say?"

"There's more?" Matthew's face contorted. "This should be interesting."

She scrambled for an explanation. "Yeah. I meant to tell you sooner. Work's been crazy, and I haven't seen you. I came up with some ideas on how we can make up for losing the contract."

"Is that why you've been avoiding me?"

Heather shrugged. "It's the beginning of the school year. I'm busy."

Matthew sat down in the chair and rolled up the papers he was carrying. "This is going to ruin the business."

"Not necessarily." Heather shifted from one foot to the other. "I said I had some ideas."

"Why didn't you tell me sooner?" Matthew asked with a gruff tone. He popped up out of the chair, letting it fall to its side, and stuffed the papers in his back pocket before pacing the length of the coop.

Queenie rushed to the wire and pecked. The hen did not like Matthew being close to her, regardless of the fact there was a barrier between them.

"I'm telling you now," Heather said. "I've been busy. When she told me last week, I wasn't—"

Matthew stomped a foot, sending a dust cloud into the air. "Last week?"

The dust tickled Heather's nose, and she sneezed. Instead of a "bless you," Matthew cursed a combination of words she'd never heard before—odd, considering where she worked and the creative nature of teenagers, but she kept that thought to herself.

"Look, Horton's will screw up, and you'll get the contract back. And Shannon said she was working on a new booster club for businesses. No one will notice when the cleaners' name isn't on the banner at the first football game."

Matthew froze. "Why won't my name be on the booster club banner?"

It crossed her mind that Brian had only shared the tip of the iceberg with her husband. That fact needed some more consideration, but right now it was damage control time.

"Any businesses with a connection to the school can't be booster club members anymore. Shannon said it's a conflict of interest."

Matthew threw his arms in the air. "All you had to do was tell me what was going on. We could have figured this out. Instead, you lied to me. Explains why you get along with Brian so well." He shook his head before he stomped toward the house.

"Wait a minute," Heather called out after him. "That's uncalled for. I didn't lie. I just didn't get around to telling you."

Halfway to the house, Matthew retorted over his shoulder, "Same thing," and kept walking.

Heather took a step toward him and stopped. He was right. She should have told him. And they couldn't discuss their options if they were fighting. Heather righted the chair and sat down. It wouldn't help to go after him when she was upset, so she sat in the quiet dusk, waiting for the elusive calm to overtake her again. An hour later, she knew she was out of luck and headed back inside to cook dinner. That would be her peace offering.

But all she found in the kitchen was a note.

Staying at the cleaners. - M

HEATHER WADDED UP THE PAPER. So much for making up. She tossed the paper in the trash and brushed away the tear that flowed down her cheek. The only bright side to the evening was that she didn't have to make dinner.

CHAPTER 13

Heather's knees clicked with each step, and her mouth was drier than the Sahara Desert. Today's run was going to kill her if the situation between her and Matthew didn't. It had been three weeks since her argument with Matthew. She suspected she was going to have to make the first move if she wanted Matthew to come home for longer than it took him to shower. But she wasn't sure what she wanted.

He was right. She should have told him. But avoiding her wasn't helping the situation. Matthew's behavior was worse than hers. How dare he judge her.

"That's the third time I've caught you mumbling to yourself," said Stacey. "What is going on?"

Heather took her gaze off the sidewalk in front of her and forced her attention to her friend.

"Sorry. Working through stuff."

Rachel laughed. "That's what you said yesterday in the teachers' lounge when you poured salt in your coffee. We know you better than that. Spill it."

"Later," Heather gasped. "After we're finished. I don't have the lung capacity." She picked up speed to position herself at the head of the group. The tears threatening to spill down her face told her she wasn't in the right frame of mind to discuss anything. Plus, crying and running were not meant to be done at the same time.

When they made it back to the parking lot, Heather had her excuse ready: she had work to do. But as she turned to her car, Stacey and Rachel linked their arms with hers, and Angela stood in front of her. Heather blew her bangs out of her eyes and twisted in a half-hearted attempt to get out of her friends' grasp. When Stacey and Rachel didn't let go, Heather slumped. "I don't want to talk about it."

"We know," said Angela, "which is exactly why we're here."

The tears dripped down Heather's face, and Angela whipped out a packet of tissues. "Are you okay?"

She stared at the tissues, then down at her arms. "I can't dry my eyes if you two keep holding my arms."

Stacey leaned forward to see Rachel's face. "Do we believe her?"

"Might as well. If she bolts, we can catch her. She's draggin' today," said Stacey.

Her friends were right. They would catch her if she made a break for it. As soon as her arms were free, she swiped a tissue from Angela and blotted her face.

"You ran five miles with barely a word—other than talking to yourself." Stacey looked at her watch. "And we had the worst split time in the last month."

"I've got a lot on my mind," said Heather, as a wave of exhaustion swept over her. She debated sitting down in the middle of the parking lot but bent over at the waist and touched her toes instead. "I'm sure I said something."

"You said *huh* whenever I asked you a question," Stacey said. "School sucks, but this is us—your friends. Tell us what's going on. Maybe we can help."

Heather whipped herself into a standing position. "How? The teachers treat me like I'm the enemy. The reason I poured salt in my coffee? Michael gave it to me when I asked him to pass the sugar." She noticed the shock on her friends' faces, but Heather couldn't help herself. It felt good to let out her frustration. "The new attendance policy gets so much pushback I don't have enough time to do anything else. I hate being the attendance czar. The kids even picked up on how much I dislike it. I bit poor Sophia Brookfield's head off when she came to make up hours."

Rachel held up a hand, as if she were a student to be called on. The absurdity of the behavior made Heather laugh, which she knew was intentional.

"Yes, Rachel. What would you like to say?"

"Why was Sophia making up time? She never misses school."

Something tickled Heather's nose, and she rubbed it. Small pieces of tissue flaked off, and she shook her head. "Thanks for letting me know I was wearing tissue on my face."

"You're welcome." Angela picked more tissue from Heather's face. "Finish telling us about Sophia."

Heather grabbed her ankle for a quad stretch. "Shannon's having the kids make up time for out-of-school activities. Sophia and the rest of the Quiz Bowl team made up five hours to leave early to attend the first tournament. Michael was furious, but Shannon said the new policy applies to all students, athletes or otherwise." She paused, switching legs. "To top it off, Matthew is still sleeping at the store. Someone's going to notice his car is always at the dry cleaners."

Heather stepped back to see what effect her tirade had left.

"He's giving you space," Stacey said.

Rachel nodded, "That's good, right?"

Heather shrugged, unsure what she wanted to hear.

Angela frowned. "I hate to be the bearer of more bad news,

but the brigade already spotted Matthew's car, from what I overhead at Betty's Coffee Bar."

"Hey, is it true Betty's making chocolate croissants?" Rachel asked.

Angela raised her eyebrows. "We're helping Heather, not feeding your sugar addiction."

"You're right." Rachel put her hands on her hips and tilted her head to the side. "Heather, I know you are getting the brunt of the work, but Shannon's changes are working. Remember how the math department was constantly hauling the social studies department to Mr. Whittaker's office to mediate their issues? They tried it once with Shannon, and she told them to figure it out themselves."

"And did they?" Heather couldn't help asking.

"It made for an entertaining conversation in the teachers' lounge, but, yep, they resolved the issue. It remains to be seen what other things they'll argue about, but for now it's all good."

Stacey wrapped her arm around Heather's shoulders. "What can we do for you?"

Heather relaxed into Stacey's hug and put her head on her friend's shoulder. "What am I supposed to do about Matthew? The situation is . . ." How much should she tell her friends? There wasn't anything they could do about it, but maybe it would be good to get it off her chest. "I don't know how we're going to make it."

"You'll find a way. You always do. We're here to help." Stacey squeezed her before letting her go. "Same time next week?"

Heather nodded, and the women walked to their respective cars. She thought the conversation was finished, but Angela pulled up next to her and rolled down the window.

"I didn't want to put you on the spot in front of Rachel and Stacey, but say the word and I'll pay Justine's tuition."

More tears threatened to spill from her eyes. Heather rubbed the back of her hand against her cheek to make sure it wasn't damp. "I can't ask you to do that. You're already done enough."

"I wouldn't offer if I didn't mean it." Angela tapped the steering wheel. "I have more clothes and cars than I need, so why not spread the wealth a bit?"

Heather reached in and covered Angela's hand with hers. As much as she wanted to figure this out on her own, Angela's offer would buy them some time until Matthew's business troubles cleared up.

"Thank you. I don't know what I'd do without you. Let me talk to Matthew, and I'll call you."

Angela's eyebrows shot up in surprise. "You're going to tell him?"

"I'm in enough trouble for not fessing up about Horton's. He's going to notice the tuition is paid in full."

Angela squeezed Heather's hand and then let go. "He never asked you how you paid for Justine's therapy and meds, did he?"

Heather felt her cheeks get warm. Her friend knew her too well.

"I told him insurance covered it all."

Angela propped her sunglasses on her forehead. "Be honest with him, Heather. If I've learned anything from being an attorney, it's that the truth is always the simplest way to go. Maybe not the easiest, but the least complicated."

Heather hobbled to her car as Angela drove away. She slid into the driver's seat and stared out the windshield. A bird flew past, making Heather envious of its freedom to do whatever it wanted, whenever it wanted. It didn't need permission. But that wasn't her situation.

Heather rested her head on the steering wheel as she considered her options. Angela was right. She needed to tell Matthew about Angela's offer to pay their daughter's tuition. But it was impossible to tell someone who wasn't there. Matthew was the one who left and hadn't bothered to call or text.

Heather sat up and made a deal with herself as she started the car. She would tell Matthew as soon as he came home. But if she needed the money before then, she was going to take Angela's offer, whether he liked it or not.

CHAPTER 14

On Thursday night, Heather discovered Matthew's dirty dishes and coffee mugs cluttering the kitchen sink when she got home from her afternoon shift of monitoring makeup attendance hours. She stacked his stuff in the dishwasher, wanting to flop on the couch. But she still had chicken duty, so she headed to the Poultry Palace.

When Heather returned to the kitchen after feeding the girls, her heart skipped a beat at the sight of Matthew sitting at the table. He didn't notice her at first. The papers strewn on the kitchen table captured his complete attention. An empty bottle of beer sat in the middle of the table, surprising her. It wasn't like Matthew to drink alone.

"Hi," she murmured as she walked to the sink and turned on the water. The warm liquid washed over her hands, and she scrubbed off the feed and dust from her evening chores. As she watched the bubbles slide down the drain, Heather struggled to remember the last time she'd enjoyed spending time with her husband. She dried her hands on the towel proclaiming Even Chickens Need a Break.

"We need to talk."

She draped the towel over the front of the sink, giving herself time to think. Heather was tired. The constant complaints from teachers, parents, and students wore her down. And now, after hiding out at the dry cleaners, Matthew wanted to talk. Avoiding each other wasn't helping, but Heather didn't have the energy for another discussion.

"Can we do it later? I still have a bunch of work to do. And I need a shower. The coop was messier than usual."

"Do you know Dr. Alexander?"

Heather jerked her hand, knocking the towel from the sink. It floated down, brushing her leg on its way to the floor. Justine had stopped seeing the doctor before she left for college, but the man was a miracle-worker. If she hadn't taken Justine to see him, Heather didn't know if their daughter would still be with them.

She bent down and picked up the towel, tilting her head to sneak a look at Matthew. He stared back at her, and her stomach clenched.

"I've heard his name. A student from the high school saw him a couple years ago." That much was true. "Why do you ask?"

He grabbed the bottle by the neck and stood up. He tossed it in the recycle bin, then opened the fridge and took out another. Only two beers remained in the six-pack.

"We've gotten some letters from him."

"Oh." Her response sounded stilted even to her.

"We owe him money." He popped the top of the beer and took a long swig. "To the tune of five thousand dollars."

"That's impossible. I paid him." The words were out of her mouth before she realized her slip. She bit the inside of her lip hard enough to taste iron. Shaking her head, Heather plopped into a chair and dropped her head into her hands. She'd avoided this discussion for more than five years. But she was so overworked from Shannon's arrival, she couldn't keep a secret.

The table rattled, and Heather peered up. Matthew slid the bottle of beer in front of her.

"I need the truth, Heather."

Heather scanned her husband's face, searching for some clue as to his current mood. She expected to find anger or irritation, but when she studied his eyes, all she saw was a tired, middle-aged man. She wished for the spark of energy or excitement that had been there before Justine got sick. But the dark bags under Matthew's eyes told her he was as tired as she was.

Heather let out a long sigh and wrapped her hands around the cold beer bottle.

"He treated Justine for about eighteen months. He's a psychiatrist who specializes in depression in teenagers. I took her to see him after she ran away her sophomore year." She sipped the beer, then pushed it back to him. This was a conversation they should have had years ago, but there wasn't anything she could do about that now.

"While I'm curious why you didn't tell me about this doctor, let's focus on the money aspect for now." He ran his hand through his hair. "Why didn't insurance cover Justine's treatment?"

"It did. Sort of."

Matthew's eyebrows lifted, and he tilted his head like he used to when Justine asked for chocolate for dinner.

"Fine. Dr. Alexander was out-of-network. Insurance covered a portion of the charges. Angela's gifts paid the rest," said Heather. She reached out and poked the papers with one finger, as if she were afraid she'd get a rash touching them. Her heart hammered when she saw the past due amounts from Dr. Alexander. "I paid the bills. I don't understand what happened."

Matthew closed his eyes and leaned back in the chair. His head fell back, and she saw the paleness of his complexion as she leaned closer to study the documents.

That's when she noticed the dates.

"These came in July. It's September. Why didn't you tell me about them before now?" Heather asked.

Matthew's eyes flew open, and she shrunk back from his penetrating blue gaze. He countered, "Why didn't you tell me our daughter was seeing a psychiatrist?"

Heather hesitated. Their marriage counselor had warned her that making decisions about their daughter's treatment without telling Matthew could undermine their marriage. *Be an open book*," the counselor recommended. Better late than never, right?

"I didn't want to fight about it. Justine needed help, and I knew you'd disagree."

What little color was left drained from Matthew's face. "You didn't tell me it was that bad."

"I tried. The best I could. But . . ." Heather let out a shaky breath. "Look, we weren't equipped to deal with her issues, and Dr. Alexander was. I got her on the waitlist, and I was going to tell you before we went. They had a last-minute opening, and you were busy at the store, and I took it. I did what was best for Justine. I figured if you ever found out you'd be okay with it. If I hadn't found help, she wouldn't be changing her major right now. Or be in college. Or even . . ." Heather trailed off, not willing to say the words.

The room fell silent. Matthew shuffled the papers while Heather steadied herself. This was her own fault, but she didn't think she'd change anything if she had to do it again.

"I tried to tell you about the bills a couple of times," said Matthew, "but you've had your hands full at work. Things are crazy at the cleaners. And obviously we don't have the greatest track record of communicating. Besides, I figured it was a mistake. Then the second statement came, so I called the office. They're happy Justine is doing well but explained there was a billing error. Somebody keyed a diagnosis code in wrong that didn't get caught until a recent audit. The office only billed half of what was really owed. They offered to set up a payment plan since I called before it went to collections." Matthew picked up the beer and drained it. "But we can't pay this. Even if the payment plan is low, we've got the mortgage and second mortgage, the car payments, the business loan, Justine's tuition."

Irritation rose in Heather's chest, but she willed herself to be calm.

"She could take out a student loan." She held up her hand when Matthew rolled his eyes. "Cybersecurity pays better than education. She could pay back the loan quickly."

Matthew shook his head. "While you have a point, we promised to pay, and I plan to deliver on that."

"Can we cover it with savings?"

Matthew stood up, the chair scraping the worn linoleum floor. The chair left a black mark, but she didn't point it out when Matthew started pacing. He never paced unless things were bad.

"Not much left after we fixed the transmission on your car." He sheepishly turned back to her. "And I also dipped in to make payroll last month."

Heather picked at her cuticle to avoid speaking. *We agreed not to do that again . . . although that's sort of hypocritical coming from me.*

Matthew ran his hands through his hair. "I figured we'd make it up when you got the new position. But since that isn't happening, we need to consider our options."

The seriousness of their predicament washed over her. It didn't seem fair that, even with a good job and a business, they couldn't make ends meet. She thought back to the night of their last fight. She propped herself onto her elbows. "You could let your employees go to reduce overhead. I can work after school and on weekends."

He cringed. "You don't have time for that. The cleaner's closed before you finish at school. And you hate working there. But that won't offset our other bills."

"I'll do it if it helps." She steadied herself before she spoke again. "Angela offered to pay Justine's tuition. I'm sure she'd pay Dr. Alexander, too, if I asked."

Heather knew Matthew's answer before the words came out of his mouth.

"We can't rely on other people to make good on our debts. Angela is your friend, not your personal banker."

She flinched but forced the words from her mouth. "She doesn't mind. Justine is like a daughter to her."

"But she's not." He held up a hand and said, "We have to take care of our own family. If we can't afford to do something, we shouldn't do it."

She let his words sink in.

"What about another mortgage? Or increase the credit line for the business?"

"Already asked. Bank said we aren't bringing in enough revenue to qualify." He reached into the fridge and pulled out the last two beers. He opened them both and handed her one before he took a long pull from the other. "The house and property have appreciated, though. We could sell and pay off everything. Even this doctor's bill."

The breath left Heather's lungs, and she swayed. She couldn't have heard Matthew right. This was their home. The place they raised their daughter. Even on their worst days, she never imagined not living in this house.

"You can't be serious." Heather gripped the table, its broken Formica edge grinding into her hand. "I don't want to leave here."

"It's that or bankruptcy. You know my stance on that."

She poked around at the papers on the table, trying to make sense of what Matthew told her. The words blurred in front of her eyes as she felt her cheeks get wet. Brushing the tears away, she shook her head.

"There has to be another option."

Matthew rested his hands on Heather's shoulders. For once, she didn't have the urge to pull away. She wanted him to wrap her in a hug and promise that everything would be okay.

"I wish there was. But, as far as I can tell, this is the best we can do." He squeezed her shoulder gently. "I'm all ears if you have a better suggestion."

Heather held the cold bottle up to her forehead and closed her eyes. She never imagined saving her daughter would result in losing the house. But it had been the right decision. Now they had to face the consequences.

"What about scholarships? Justine would be eligible for a fresh set of them with her new major."

Matthew dropped his hands and sat down. "Even if she got the money, it wouldn't be in time."

Desperation forced her to make the next suggestion. "I could ask my mom. She's always talking about saving for a rainy day."

Matthew snorted. "Have you even told her Justine changed her major?"

Heather closed her eyes. Even though selling the house was the only immediate solution, she didn't want to. There had to be another way. But since she didn't have an obvious solution right now, Heather could explore the possibility while she looked for something else. How bad could it be?

CHAPTER 15

"I'm so excited about selling your house!"

Heather stifled a groan at the same time Matthew coughed. It had been a week since they hired Delores "Call me Dot" Morris. Dot seemed like the answer to their problems, even if she was a little over-the-top for Heather's taste. The teased, bleached hair and hot-pink lipstick reminded Heather more of a Dolly Parton impersonator than a real estate agent. But Dot was a long-time resident of Stadium, a top seller in the area, and gossip brigade approved. Heather ground her teeth when she thought about the next time she ran into Mrs. Hunsinger, but she pushed that aside.

"I hope you two aren't coming down with something. You've got a lot of work to do to get this place shipshape and ready to sell." She put a stapled stack of paper in front of each of them. "Now, don't get overwhelmed when you see the to-do list. Yours is more of a medium-length list. Some clients have thirty pages. You have ten."

Heather swallowed the nausea Dot's enthusiasm caused. She skimmed the list and forced herself to listen as Dot extolled the virtues of neutralizing a home. "A potential buyer needs to feel comfortable. They need to imagine their furnishings in your space. It's important to remove personal items like family pictures and collectibles. Just because you see the quaintness of presidential spoons doesn't mean your potential buyer has an interest in seeing them on the wall."

"What's quaint about spoons?" Heather murmured. Matthew poked her. She glanced sideways at Matthew, who raised his eyebrows. "I was just asking."

"We've been cleaning," Matthew said. "We'll be ready to go next week."

Dot flung back her head, sending the flamingos on her dangling earrings flying into her hair as if they were burying their heads in the sand, and laughed hysterically. When Dot settled down, she dabbed at her wet eyes and said, "Matthew, dear, this house needs more attention than what you can give it in a week. I expect it will take a month or more before it's ready to be staged, let alone good enough for an open house."

Matthew's eyes bulged like they would pop out of his head. "We don't have a month." He flipped through the pages. "And we don't have the money for this. We want to sell the house, not fix it up for someone else."

Dot squirmed in her seat, something Heather resisted. She wished Matthew hadn't told the agent how desperate they were.

"You have to spend money to make money." She nodded to the walls. "You're behind the times on wall color. Gray is dull and boring. Pale-yellow is where it's at. I can't imagine anyone wanting to buy this place as it is now. Excuse my bluntness, but if you want to sell this, you have some work to do."

"I can put in the work, but I'm not putting in a bunch of money." Matthew tossed the list onto the coffee table. "Maximum profit with as little financial investment as possible."

"But I can get you more if you update! The kitchen counters, for example, are chipped. Installing new ones immediately elevates the look of the room. That's item fourteen."

"What can we do that costs nothing but will make the house more appealing?" Heather skimmed down the list in front of her. "There have to be some things we can do for free."

Dot wrinkled her nose as if being served a block of Limburger. "Dear, I don't think you understand. This house needs work if you want me to sell it at top dollar."

"We don't care about top dollar. Average works. It needs to be fast."

The agent's sigh rivaled that of a teenager being told to read a book instead of scroll social media. "Anything from items seventy-five on won't cost you anything. But I caution against ignoring the other items. The paint in here needs to be done." She shuddered as if the paint was personally offending. "I don't think I can work with gray. It's so 2010."

Heather wondered what Dot would say if she told her the walls were white but layered with years of dirt and dust. Washing the walls wasn't something she wanted added to the to-do list. "Is it necessary to go through all the kitchen cabinets and closets? Why does anyone care what I have if the doors are closed?"

That question earned her a ten-minute lecture on the illusion of space and how buyers needed to be convinced there was room for their stuff, even if there wasn't. "It's all about making people comfortable. Which reminds me—what's the plan for the chickens?"

Heather frowned, confused by the question. "They'll move with us. I'm not selling them with the house. Or the coop, for that matter."

"No, dear." Dot snickered. "I meant when are you removing them from the property? Unless you're selling a farm, no one expects livestock."

Matthew shrugged. "They have to go at some point. Might as well deal with it now. We won't have space in an apartment. It'd free up your evenings, too."

Heather ignored Dot's triumphant snort and leaned toward her husband. She knew they'd downsize, but not that much. "An apartment?"

"Have you seen the price of houses these days? By the time we pay off everything, we won't have much for a down payment. An apartment is our best option. Maybe our *only* option."

"They're part of the family." Heather stood up and walked to the window where she could see the coop. "I don't want to get rid of the chickens."

Matthew said, "And I don't want to move."

"Excuse me, but you've hired me to sell the house. I'm telling you how to do that," Dot said. "Someone will want the chickens. Fresh eggs are much better than the store-bought ones."

"No argument there," said Matthew. He glanced at Heather when he added, "But a chicken and an egg are two entirely different things."

The real estate agent cocked her head as if she had missed something. "Is that supposed to be a joke?"

Heather recognized Matthew's attempt at humor, but she wasn't ready to laugh. She caught sight of Queenie out the window, scratching in the dirt. It would be easier without the chickens, but they brought her peace and joy. She'd lost enough with her work situation. Why should she give up the only thing that brought her peace and joy?

"Can we sell the house first, then figure out what to do with the chickens?" Heather asked, expecting an argument.

Matthew ran his hands through his hair and turned to Dot. "What do you think?"

Dot surprised Heather when she picked up the to-do list and

said, "If you're keeping the chickens, then item number eighteen is nonnegotiable. Deal?"

Matthew looked at Heather. She checked the list and rolled her eyes. She knew she sounded like a child when she said, "Deal."

CHAPTER 16

tem eighteen: Interior walls painted butter-yellow. Check.

Heather shoved Dot's checklist into her briefcase and assessed her desk. The pile of attendance slips needed attention, but all she wanted to do was put her head down and take a catnap. She'd painted past midnight and was up at five. Heather was burning the candle at both ends and didn't know how much longer her body could take it.

She yawned as she grabbed the slips. Francine in the front office was supposed to enter them into the system, but she complained she was too busy. She'd been too busy since school started. Usually, Heather didn't mind doing it, but today she wished she'd never offered to help.

On the positive side of things, the guidance counselor was coming by in fifteen minutes to discuss the letters of reference Heather had offered to write for this year's senior class. She'd also volunteered to read through application essays so the students would have two different critiques. After that, she was headed to the Stadium Diner for lunch with Angela. Her friend was helping her with truancy issues, but at least Heather got to see a friendly face. Prepping a house to sell and being the attendance czar drained the joy out of her days.

Heather entered three attendance slips into the system before she noticed the yellow paint stuck under her nails. Stacey had warned her to wear gloves, but she forgot last night. She'd been so tired; all she wanted to do was finish and go to bed. Heather leaned over the trash can and picked out the paint, flicking it into the can while she wondered if the work was worth it.

The point of selling the house was to generate some much-needed money. That's why she and Matthew were doing as much on their own as possible. To be fair, Matthew was helping too. It was a nice change for the two of them to work side by side and not argue. But the constant list of repairs, improvements, and cleaning projects from Dot was tilting her emotional balance in the wrong direction.

"Mrs. Ramsey, do you have a minute?"

Heather whipped up her head at the sound of Shannon's voice. Despite the principal's appointment policy, Heather discovered it only worked in one direction. Shannon had no qualms about dropping in unannounced, although usually the clicking of her heels gave her away.

"I have a few minutes before my next meeting." Heather flicked another paint chip into the trash can, then turned her full attention to the principal. "What can I do for you?"

Shannon nodded and took a step into Heather's office. "The guidance counselor and I met earlier today. She told me about your meeting. I cancelled it."

She felt like the school bully had just stolen her lunch money, but Heather forced herself to stay calm. She knew what happened when someone reacted to Shannon. Michael had raised his voice defending the Quiz Bowl team during a staff meeting and spent two days at home on unpaid leave.

This was the third time this week Shannon had interfered

with her calendar. Granted, the woman was her boss and had the authority to tell her what to do. She admitted Shannon's intervention had saved her from two heated meetings with football parents wanting her to fudge the attendance policy so their sons could play in Friday's game. But Heather was looking forward to meeting with the guidance counselor.

"May I ask why?"

Shannon crossed her arms and leaned against the door frame.

"The counseling office is responsible for college prep activities. You've helped in the past, but considering your new assignments, I want you to focus on your own work. There are still some teachers not using the digital textbooks; that's yours to implement. I also noticed there continue to be dress code infractions. We don't need any more high schoolers off leash. They know the rules. Lead them in the right direction."

A groan threatened to escape Heather's lips, but she swallowed it down and said, "I have the bandwidth for it. I don't mind." Heather knew she didn't have the time or energy, but if she didn't have something fun to look forward to, she might act out like the students, who were forced to change out of inappropriate T-shirts or remove their hats.

Heather noticed Shannon's hair didn't move as she walked into the office and picked up the stack of attendance slips. Cocking her head to one side, she frowned. "Why are these on your desk?"

"They need to be entered into the system."

Shannon raised her eyebrow, and Heather squirmed in her seat. "You are the vice principal."

Heather winced at Shannon's statement, then said quietly, "Front desk hasn't been able to get around to it."

"Unacceptable. These slips are antiquated. It's the teachers' responsibility to input classroom attendance. That's the policy, which you can enforce. So, enforce it."

A wave of exhaustion hit her, and before she knew it, Heather said, "With all due respect, it doesn't work that way."

"Because you won't let it," said Shannon as she sat down in the chair across from Heather and took in the state of Heather's desk. The stern expression dropped from her face, and Heather thought she saw a look of concern on Shannon's face. "I'm new, and I'm changing things. But from where I'm sitting, you're overwhelmed. Part of my job is to help you. Letting you focus on your job is a good thing."

Heather forced a smile. "I appreciate it. But I like working with the kids on college applications. Plus, it puts another set of eyes on their work. Everything counts during the process."

"You may enjoy it, but the counseling office is on its own for the college applications. Which reminds me, what is this all about?" Shannon held out a business card, and Heather grimaced. "I got it from a girl wearing a T-shirt from a local bar and jeans that had more holes than fabric. When I asked her to report to the office for replacement clothing, she gave me this. A get-out-of-jail-free card for dress code infractions is creative but useless."

"I've confiscated a few of those myself. The culprit has been dealt with." Heather hoped. The family and consumer sciences teacher swore she wouldn't make any new cards, but there was no telling how many were still circulating. "There has been some issue with the 'no holes in clothes' policy. It might be better to amend the policy and recommend church wear."

Shannon's back stiffened. "We're a public school."

"I know. But students and parents understand what we expect if we word it that way."

Shannon shook her head. "The policy should read there are to be no holes in any clothes worn to school or school functions —jeans, tops, dresses, or otherwise."

"We need to tweak that. The debate team loves a technicality.

Someone will argue modern clothing *requires* holes to wear it. We don't want the student body showing up in togas."

Shannon snorted.

For the first time in her boss's presence, Heather relaxed. Shannon was human after all.

"*Touché.*" Shannon coughed in her hand to recover before she stood up. "Thank you. I never would have seen that coming." From the doorway, Shannon said, "Make the changes you see fit and send them to me. I'm heading back to the front office. I'll let Francine know you'll be in to discuss the attendance slips." She paused and studied Heather. "It really is easier to deal with things now versus later. Trust me on that one."

Shannon wasn't wrong, Heather thought as she watched her leave. It was in her power to ask for help. But some people didn't appreciate change. Heather certainly didn't like the fact that the dry cleaners was no longer working with the school. There wasn't anything she could do about it, so she'd accepted it and moved on. But old-timers like Francine did not embrace change. When it came from outsiders, they fought against it.

Maybe she should detour to Brian's office for some football pads. She might need them.

CHAPTER 17

"You're late," Angela said. "That's not like you."

Heather fell into the seat across from her friend and accepted the box of sweetener Angela pushed toward her. A glass, sweating from the cold iced tea inside, waited expectantly. She yanked her purse from her shoulder and took a second to smooth down her hair. She hated running behind, especially with Angela.

"Francine and I are currently engaged in a battle of wills."

"Who's Francine?"

"Admin assistant." Heather dug through the box to find two sweetener packets she liked. "Although she isn't really assisting anyone."

"Never battle with the help. It always ends badly. What's the issue?"

Stirring the sugar into her tea, Heather sighed. "I asked her to do her job."

Angela nodded. "Sounds reasonable. Typically, employees have a set of responsibilities they are required to do. What's the issue with that?"

"I've never made her do anything for me before." Heather

drained half of the iced tea and slumped back, waiting for the sugar to jumpstart her system. She saw the amusement on Angela's face and groaned. "I know. It's my own fault, which I have been reminded of several times by Shannon."

"That goes in her favor." Angela sipped her water, then asked, "What exactly is Francine not doing?"

Heather dropped her chin to her chest, hoping to release the built-up tension in her neck. "In this instance, the attendance slips. At first, she refused to enter them. Then she entered them wrong."

Angela's face puckered as if she'd sucked on the lemon that was garnishing her water. "That does not bode well for our discussion on how to prepare for truancy hearings. Most judges like things neat and orderly. Bad recordkeeping is not viewed favorably."

The server arrived at the table, and they ordered their usual: meatloaf for Heather and a turkey club sandwich for Angela.

"I asked her to redo them," Heather said, "which sent her into a lecture of how my father would be disappointed I was cowing to the new principal, who is, among other things, an outsider."

"She has a point."

Heather frowned, but Angela shrugged.

"Well, she does. The outsider part of it." Angela checked the text message that popped up on her phone before putting it back in her purse. "How did you finally get her to do the work?"

Heather grimaced. "Shannon. I wish I'd captured Francine's face on video when Shannon asked her what the problem was." Heather hitched her voice an octave lower. "Oh, nothing Principal Parker. Just taking some direction from Heather." Heather's voice pitched up, imitating Shannon. "I believe that's Mrs. Ramsey.'"

Angela threw up a hand. "That explains the battle of wills."

"Francine is no longer speaking to me, which is fine—if she fixes the entries. Let's talk about something less depressing."

Heather pulled out a notepad. "Truancy officer duties. Here's my list of questions. Things are a little foggy to me. Can you walk me through them?"

The process was more straightforward than Heather thought it would be. Angela produced a flowchart for her to follow. Even though it contained more than fifty steps, it made sense. By the time lunch arrived, Heather felt better about her role as attendance czar.

"Your superpower is explaining things. Where were you when we took physics in high school?"

"Failing alongside you. Science is my kryptonite." Angela took a bite of her sandwich before asking, "How are things going with the house? Is it on the market yet?"

Heather pushed an onion out of her salad before stabbing a black olive with her fork. "Dot seems to think we're almost ready. The big issue is the chickens."

Angela shook her head. "I will help with anything but those silly chickens."

"I know. But I don't want to get rid of them. They make me happy."

"You should try shoe shopping. That works for me."

"Shopping requires money."

Angela reached into her bag and pulled out an envelope. She slid it across the table. "Ask and ye shall receive."

Heather gripped her fork tighter, her fingers itching to take the money. Accepting Angela's help in the past had solved one problem but created another. She remembered how nice things were last night. She and Matthew had painted the living room side by side, talking about the mundane and not fighting once. If Heather took this money, would it destroy any hope for their marriage?

Heather pushed back the envelope. "We need to figure this out on our own."

"Even if it means giving up your precious chickens?"

The thought of rehoming her five girls made her sad. And angry. She didn't want to get rid of the one thing that made her happy and kept her dad's memory close. But she didn't have to make the choice now.

"Yes. When we get back on our feet, I can get more."

"But you won't. You're always sacrificing things you love." Angela nudged the envelope forward again. "If you won't take it for yourself, take it for Justine. It won't pay all her tuition, but it'll put a dent in it. Although you could use a shopping trip. The school attendance officer appears in court regularly. A golf shirt and capris will not cut it. You need a suit and nice heels."

"Why do that when I can borrow your clothes?" But Heather put the envelope in her purse. As soon as she got home, she'd tell Matthew. She could always give it back to Angela if Matthew fussed, but she hoped she wouldn't have to. "Thank you. Justine says thank you, too."

The attorney wiped her hands on a napkin. "You are welcome. I personally hope you are leaning toward a shopping trip."

"I don't see that happening anytime soon, but I'm okay with wishful thinking." Heather glanced at her watch before waving over their server. "Time to head back and see if Francine has come up with my punishment."

"Go ahead. I've got lunch." Angela handed her credit card to the server before Heather could argue. "For the record, I agree with Shannon. Let Francine do her job. You do yours. This isn't what you wanted, but you're getting a handle on things now."

On Heather's drive back to school, she mulled over what Angela had said. Maybe Shannon was right, but it stung a bit that Angela had sided with the principal. Her friend meant well, but it would be nice if Angela would stop being logical occasionally.

She chuckled. That would never happen.

By the next week, Francine had gotten the hang of the attendance slips. She had also started talking to Heather again.

"My daughter wants to raise chickens. She'll take the hens off your hands when you're ready."

Heather smiled, ignoring the wave of sadness Francine's comment triggered. Finding a suitable home for her chickens would whittle down Heather's to-do list, but she didn't like the thought of life without Queenie.

"I'll get back to you on that," she said as she headed back to her office.

She jostled through the crowded hallways, nodding and waving at students as she went. The students had taken the recent changes in stride. Heather didn't spot any holes in clothing, and everyone enjoyed more conversation time with friends since they didn't have to stop at lockers for their books.

The hallway noise was so loud, though, that she missed a call from Matthew. She closed her office door and listened to the message.

"Dot changed her mind about the yellow we used in the living room and wants us to repaint. I told her no. If she calls you, tell her no. Bye."

Heather grinned. It was too soon to tell, but she thought things were turning around between the two of them.

She forced herself to focus on work. Heather checked for other voicemail messages and, when she didn't find any, she turned her attention to her email. Angela's flowchart had revealed four football players who were prime candidates for truancy court. Despite repeated calls and emails to their parents, asking them to contact her, no one had acknowledged her requests.

Heather leaned her head back on her chair. She examined the ceiling as she considered how to tell Brian he was losing his offensive line. And less than a month before the homecoming game. She decided she would go find him in the weight room after school.

"Knock, knock." The smell of the coffee hit her olfactory senses, and she looked over to see Brian holding a carrier with two cups of coffee and two pastry bags. So much for having to track him down. "Ya have a minute?"

"If you brought me an almond *pain au chocolat* along with a macchiato, I'll give you an hour."

The coach's laugh filled the room as he walked in and handed off the goodies. "Things that bad, huh?"

Heather took a sip of the coffee, in awe of its perfect temperature, before she opened a pastry bag and pulled out the still warm French delicacy. She took a bite, and it melted in her mouth. This was why she put up with Stacey's long runs. These carbs might be calorie-dense but tasted amazing. The sugar and caffeine pepped her up, and she said to Brian, "You tell me. You've got four football players who won't make the game against Glen Valley due to attendance issues. Their parents aren't responding to calls or emails, and they haven't shown up for makeup sessions."

Brian's eyebrows rose. "That's homecoming."

She took another sip of her coffee and nodded. As much as she wanted to help Brian, there wasn't much she could do if the boys or their parents weren't willing to meet her halfway.

"This new principal certainly knows how to be a buzzkill. Who are they?"

"Blake, Hudson, TJ, and Miguel."

Heather didn't like Shannon that much, but the principal was only doing her job. Someone needed to get the football team to follow the rules. Instead of pointing that out, Heather bit into her pastry.

"TJ is on the homecoming court. What do you do about that?"

Heather swallowed the food. "He'll be removed. We'll have three candidates instead of four. The fact that the homecoming court and the offensive line are affected doesn't matter."

"And if I get them to the makeup sessions? What then?"

"Depends on how many hours they get in. TJ and Hudson each need seven hours. It would take them two weeks of after-school sessions. They could be eligible before homecoming." Heather glanced at the spreadsheet still pulled up on her monitor. "But Miguel is missing twelve hours, and Blake fifteen. There aren't enough scheduled sessions to accommodate all that time."

Brian gazed over her shoulder and drummed his fingers on her desk. Heather recognized this as his thinking mode, so she focused on her coffee and pastry. She didn't enjoy delivering bad news, but the chocolate soothed her soul.

"What about Saturdays?"

She dabbed the corner of her mouth. "What about them?"

"Can you schedule makeup sessions on Saturdays? There are three Saturdays before homecoming. The guys could go to those, still attend practice, and fulfill Shannon's new rules." Brian took a sip of his coffee and leaned back in the chair. "That's a win for everyone."

Heather shook an image of five high schoolers dancing in a library out of her head. Sitting at the school on a weekend sounded horrible. It was also impossible. "I appreciate the suggestion, but I man the counter at the dry cleaners on Saturdays." She ignored the fact that Matthew had said he didn't need her.

Brian put his coffee cup on her desk and leaned forward. "How are you two making things work after the assisted living facility canceled its contract? I heard they got a better deal from Horton's."

The pastry dropped like a rock in her stomach. Matthew had mentioned nothing to her about losing another contract. Heather swallowed the now tasteless flakes and said, "As far as I know, we still have that contract."

"The gossip brigade was all over it this morning." He stood up and took his coffee. "Maybe they're wrong."

The brigade was never wrong, but Heather stayed silent. Maybe things weren't better between her and Matthew. He would have told her about this, wouldn't he? She pushed away the rest of the pastry and considered her options. Matthew didn't want her help, and if the offensive line was benched, the football team didn't have a chance. She might as well solve the school's problems since she couldn't solve her own.

"If I can make Saturdays work, can you get the players there?"

"My boys will be there. Let me know when and where."

She wanted to be irritated with Brian's confidence, but she wasn't. Life would be easier if she could be more like him.

Heather realized her mood must be obvious when Brian asked, "Something else bothering ya?"

Heather picked at her pastry. "I'm no longer allowed to write student recommendation letters. It isn't in my department."

"You love those, Sugar," Brian said. He leaned forward in his chair. "Plus, you're good at them."

"Thank you. That's not all of it, though." She knew he'd hear the news eventually. "We're selling the house, and it's been a process getting it ready to put on the market. The real estate agent and I aren't seeing eye to eye."

"She wants you to get rid of the chickens, doesn't she?"

Heather nodded.

"If you want another agent, I can recommend a couple. They aren't from around here, but they could still help. They've got billboards all over the county and were the top sellers in their group last year."

A sip of coffee helped her swallow her embarrassment, and she shook her head.

"It's okay. Matthew likes Dot, and she's not that bad. She just doesn't like my chickens. But thanks for the offer."

"Anytime. I need to get back at it, but here's my latest report." Brian pulled an envelope from his back pocket and handed it to her. "The superintendent requested you keep hand-delivering it. Please."

Heather pointed at the empty pastry bag. "Aha! This was a bribe!"

"Maybe." Brian winked at her. "But it worked, right?"

"Sure, but only because I'll be there anyway."

Brian's brows raised. "Oh, really? What other business do you have with the superintendent?"

"I'm dropping off some broken tablets to the IT department. I can swing by the super's office after."

Heather put the rest of her uneaten pastry in the bag, crumpled it, and tossed it toward the trash can. The bag hit the edge and bounced onto the floor. Brian bent down and picked it up before dropping it in the can.

"Best you stick with admin work. Your shooting skills leave something to be desired."

Heather picked up her coffee cup and aimed it at him. "I'd get out of here if I were you."

Brian laughed as he headed out the door.

CHAPTER 19

*H*eather groaned. She'd scoured the district office, but the superintendent was nowhere to be found. Heather returned to the reception desk to find out if Regina knew where he was.

"Man's been scarce these days. Ever since they hired that Dallas woman, it's been awful quiet around here. Board of Education's keepin' a low profile too. Somethin' feels off, but you never know about elected officials these days. Lookin' out for number one."

Heather didn't have time to talk politics. She'd decided to surprise Matthew at the cleaners and help him close. It was the least she could do since he took care of Dot. She glanced at her watch. Unless she left right now, it wasn't going to happen.

Regina continued. "But the school's runnin' better. Guess you have to be the bad guy sometimes to get things done. She's not supervillain bad, mind ya. An outsider, yes, but she's got her ducks in a row."

"I agree with that." Heather hesitated. She shouldn't leave the report with Regina, but she didn't have time to hang around.

Heather dug into her purse and pulled out an envelope. "Regina, would you mind—"

The front door opened before she could finish her sentence. When Heather saw the principal heading their way, she panicked. She stuffed the envelope back into her purse, only she missed the pocket. The envelope made an audible *splat* when it hit the floor, and Heather froze. She'd grabbed the envelope from Angela, not Brian. She didn't know which was worse for the principal to find—an envelope full of cash or Brian's reports she wasn't supposed to deliver.

Before Heather could recover, Shannon stopped in front of her and retrieved the envelope.

"Here you are, Mrs. Ramsey," Shannon said. "I wasn't expecting to see you here this afternoon."

Heather took the envelope and dropped it quickly into her purse before pulling out Brian's delivery for the superintendent. She handed it to Regina. "Just dropping off something that got misdelivered. Can you get this to the right place?"

Regina glanced at the recipient's name and gave Heather an odd look before she nodded.

"Thank you." Heather didn't know what she would have done if Regina asked questions. Rather than stick around and find out, Heather headed for the door. She called out over her shoulder, "Good night," then dashed to her car.

By the time Heather pulled into the cleaners, her heart rate had slowed, and she convinced herself Shannon didn't know what had happened. Heather jumped out of the car, but she paused at the sight of the closed sign on the door. Her shoulders slumped. She was too late to surprise her husband. She checked the door anyway and found it was still unlocked.

Heather rushed to the back room, where she expected to find mounds of clothes ready to be sorted and processed, but she stopped short.

Empty sorting bins lined the walls in neat rows. The dry-cleaning machine sat empty, and the pressing area was silent. Two clothing racks stood half full of plastic-wrapped garments ready to be picked up. Another ten racks stood empty. The floor sparkled, a sign it had been swept and mopped.

A chill ran down Heather's back. "Matthew! What's going on?"

Matthew popped his head out of the corner office.

"Hey. Why are you here?"

"I came to surprise you."

Matthew walked into the back room and shook his head. "I'm surprised."

Her eyes narrowed. "What's going on here? It's too early to have the store this clean."

Matthew waved around the room. "I don't think we can put off the house sale much longer. This is the third day in a row I've finished before close."

The chill spread from her back to her hands and feet. This was bad. Maybe Brian was right. She looked at the folding tables, which were completely empty.

"Where are the sheets from the assisted living facility?"

Matthew looked away. "They didn't send anything this week."

"Why is that?" She held her breath. Surely her husband would have mentioned something, considering all the problems they were having. When he didn't answer, she knew Brian was right. "Matthew? Why didn't they send anything this week?"

"They cancelled the contract. The manager told me he didn't have a choice. If we don't support the booster club, they can't support us. I told you this would happen."

She threw her hands up in the air. "And yet it was Brian who told me about the contract."

Matthew's face reddened. "Your ex-boyfriend sure goes out of his way to keep you informed."

"As my husband, isn't that *your* job?" She dug out the envelope Angela had given her the previous week and tossed it on the folding station. "And it's my job as your wife to come up with solutions. Here's a solution."

Even though they could no longer afford marriage counseling, Heather knew what Dr. Austen would say about her behavior: *"Pushing Matthew isn't going to make things better."* But Heather was tired of playing nice.

"What is it?" Matthew asked.

"What do you think it is? Money. Cash that we can use to stop the hemorrhaging."

Her husband approached the envelope slowly, as though assessing whether it contained anything dangerous. She could tell the minute he recognized Angela's handwriting on the front, because he immediately stepped away from it like he'd stumbled on a rattlesnake.

"No. Absolutely not. We've already had this discussion."

"You had it. We have friends who want to help—"

Matthew interrupted, "Friends can't pay our bills forever. We have to take control of our lives and figure it out. Just like you can't run to your ex-boyfriend every time we have a fight."

The temperature in the room seemed to drop several degrees.

"What did you say?"

"You heard me. The entire town knows you still like Brian. Why that's news to you is beyond me."

"For the record, I don't go to Brian. He comes to me." The comment had sounded better in her head, but she couldn't take it back. "Besides, I married you. Not him. I stuck with marriage counseling after you said it was a waste of time. And I'd still be going if we had the money."

"You talk a good talk, and yet you hang out with a man who hates me."

Heather rolled her eyes.

Matthew continued, "Go ahead. Act like I'm exaggerating. But you know as well as I do that the only person he cares about is himself. Did you stop to ask why he would go out of his way to tell you about the contract?"

Heather hesitated. Brian showed up at the most opportune times. But he had a legitimate reason for being there. It didn't hurt that he brought her treats, but thinking about it made it seem a little off.

She swallowed back her uncertainty. Heather refused to admit to Matthew that she had questions, too, especially since part of the reason she was late tonight was because of Brian. She shook her head. This argument was old news, and it wasn't helping the current situation.

"No. I didn't. I'm too busy wondering why you didn't tell me yourself." She left the money on the station and stomped to the front of the store. "I'm going home. If you aren't going to use the money, then I've got more work to do. With all this extra time, I might as well work on the house."

She made it to her car when Matthew followed her out, calling her name.

"Why did she really give you this money?" He pulled the envelope from his back pocket and held it out to her. "Tell me the truth."

Heather looked down her nose at the one thing that should have made their night better. "Angela wants to help. She told me to go shopping, but I told her no." She paused before adding, "I'm not a completely selfish person."

"I never said you were." He took a step closer and put the envelope in her hand. "Tell Angela thank you, but we have to do this on our own."

Heather watched Matthew turn around and walk back into the dry cleaners. He locked the door, turned off the front lights, and disappeared into the back. The darkness of the store matched Heather's mood as she got into the car and turned toward home. She might as well use her manic energy for something positive.

CHAPTER 20

"You could have told your mom the timing is bad with your new responsibilities," Matthew said as he placed a sterling-silver fork next to a gold-edged bone china plate. Heather's mother demanded formal place settings in the dining room for her semi-annual visits. "Because it is. The house is finally ready for Dot, and we can't afford to wait any longer."

Heather set a crystal water goblet above the plate and sighed. Matthew was right. Instead of relaxing, she had spent the bulk of her October break deep-cleaning the house and juggling phone calls from creditors. When the bank called to say their account was overdrawn, Matthew reluctantly deposited the cash Angela had given them. Heather expected the bump in their balance to improve the situation, but she worried it wasn't enough.

"If I push back now, Mom will know something is up. It's only for a few days while Justine is back for break. Mom will be gone by Sunday."

"Better be. Dot's putting the sign in the yard on Monday, and the showing is Tuesday. She thinks we can get the full asking price and have the house sold by Christmas."

The thought of celebrating the holidays someplace else made Heather sad. She remembered Dr. Austen's advice after Justine graduated from high school: *"Each new beginning has new traditions."* But Heather struggled to apply the advice to this situation. Twenty-five years in this house was a long time.

By Thursday night, Heather's nerves were frazzled. She seated her mother in the dining room while Justine and Matthew brought out the food. Heather had planned the meal with everyone's favorite dishes to prevent complaining. She dove into her prepared conversation list as soon as everyone had filled their plates.

"How's pickleball going?" she asked her mother. With any luck, Ruth would spend the next twenty minutes pontificating about the sport. "Is Marge still your partner?"

Her mother looked at her like she had sprouted two heads. "Of course. What's gotten into you?" Ruth took a bite of potato salad. "The house looks so clean and organized. You're like that lady who babbles about finding joy in your possessions."

"Yeah, Mom," Justine agreed. "My bedroom's clean, too. What did you do with my stuffed animals?"

Before Heather could think of a reason for decluttering the house—other than for selling it—Matthew piped up, "It's time to thin things out around here. We boxed up the animals if you want them. If not, your mom found a charity that will take them. Same with the clothes you never wear and the books you read when you were in middle school. Someone else would enjoy having them if you don't want them anymore."

Heather made a mental note to thank Matthew later.

Ruth said through a mouthful of potato salad, "Should have done that years ago, if you ask me."

Justine laid down her fork and placed her hands on the table.

When she didn't speak immediately, Heather's stomach clenched. The semester had gone off without a hitch. Even the heavier class load for Justine's new cybertechnology major had been a nonissue. Her daughter radiated happiness. Was her mother going to ruin Justine's evening with her snarky comments?

"I might go through the boxes and pick one or two things for keepsakes, but the rest you can give away." Justine picked up her fork and speared a piece of meat. "Thanks for asking me, though. It's nice to be treated like an adult."

Heather smoothed the napkin she'd unconsciously crumbled, proud of Justine's placidity.

"You *are* an adult," Ruth said as she concentrated on the green beans on her plate. "It's about time you were treated like one. You will be educating young minds soon, so you better get ready for it."

Heather froze. She hadn't told her mother about Justine's major change, and she'd hoped to keep it under wraps for a few more months, at least until the house sold and their financial lives were back in order.

Before she could intervene, Justine turned to her and frowned. "Why didn't you tell Grandma I switched majors?"

"You did what?" Ruth's fork clattered to the plate as her voice pitched up three octaves. "How could you break a family tradition?"

Heather placed her hand on Justine's. "I'm proud of you for making your own decision. I didn't tell Grandma because she . . . well, because I knew this would be her reaction."

Justine pulled her hand away from Heather's and sat up straighter. "Grandma, I'm not interested in being a teacher. It's a thankless job—you work constantly for a third of what you're worth. I'm studying cybersecurity now and already have a paid internship lined up for the summer. The position is in demand, and my professor says I'm a natural."

"That's great news, honey," said Heather. She wanted to hug

her daughter, but it was clear from the look on Justine's face that it wouldn't be welcomed.

Ruth pushed back from the table. She glared at Heather, making Heather feel like a teenager caught drinking a beer in the high school parking lot, before returning her stare to Justine.

"This is not acceptable. You are a fifth-generation teacher. It's bad enough your mother lost out on the principal position, but the Board of Education will rectify its mistake when they see what a mess this outsider makes."

"Mom, it doesn't work like that. Shannon's contract runs—"

Ruth waved away Heather's comment. "I don't care about contracts. That woman has no business coming into this town and taking over." She focused on Justine. "Just like you have no business outside of teaching. Besides, cybersecurity is too hard for someone with your problems."

Tears filled Justine's eyes.

Heather pushed back from the table, stood up, and rushed to her daughter's aid.

"Justine does not have problems. She has a condition that she is treating. Just like your diabetes."

"I'm better now, and I can do whatever I set my mind to." Justine grabbed hold of her mother's arm and pulled her back down. "Is that why you didn't tell Grandma? Because you don't think I can do it either?"

Matthew interjected, "No. Like your mom said, we didn't tell Ruth because we knew this would happen. We'd rather have dinner without a bunch of yelling and screaming."

Heather raised a hand, hoping to calm everyone, when a movement outside caught her attention. Dot's blue sedan had pulled up in front of the house, and the real estate agent got out of the car. Heather's stomach fell as Dot jogged around to the back of the car and popped open the trunk.

Heather frantically looked at her husband, who rose from

his seat at the same time she asked, "Matthew, can you see what's going on outside?" Maybe he could stop Dot before she revealed their secret.

"What's gotten into you two?" her mother asked. "Interrupting dinner is poor manners."

If Dot placed a For Sale sign in the yard now, things were going to get a lot worse than Ruth complaining about etiquette.

"Not now, Mom. I need to take care of something."

Heather leapt up and followed Matthew to the door. He wrenched it open, but it was too late. Dot carried the bright-yellow sign in her hands as she walked into the yard.

"What's she doing, Mom?" Justine asked from behind her.

"We were going to tell you, honey," Heather called back over her shoulder, "but we didn't have a chance."

"Tell her what?" asked Ruth as she flanked Heather. "Why is there a woman in your front yard?"

At that moment, Dot saw them on the porch and waved. The sign turned so they could read it, and Heather heard Justine's cry and her mother's oath.

"You're selling the house and didn't tell me?" Justine cried. "So much for treating me like an adult!"

Ruth's voice trembled when she said, "Heather, there better be a good explanation for this."

"I guess you didn't get my message," said Dot, her voice subdued from its normal upbeat nature.

"No, we've been busy," Matthew said. "You're not supposed to be here until Monday."

Justine crossed her arms over her chest. "Mother, you have some explaining to do."

"Yes, young lady, you do." Ruth wrapped her arms around Justine. "We both deserve to know what's going on."

CHAPTER 21

When everyone stepped into the yard, the real estate agent introduced herself. "Hello, everyone. My name is Delores Morris, but everyone calls me—"

Ruth interrupted, "Dot. I know who you are. I used to live here. My question is, what are you doing in my daughter's front yard? This property is not for sale."

"It will be as of Tuesday morning. We have considerable interest in it as well. Three agents heard about it and have asked for showings." She smiled, the smear of her hot-pink lipstick prominent on her two front teeth. "That's on top of Tuesday's scheduled showing and the open house. With this much interest, you could get above asking price."

Justine stepped out of her grandmother's grasp and rushed toward Heather. She put her hand on her mom's arm. "Are you doing this because of me?"

Heather searched Justine's face for any sign of panic or distress, but all she could see were questions. She glanced at Matthew, who gave her a quick nod, before turning back to her daughter.

"Yes and no."

Justine crossed her arms. "You didn't let me get away with that answer as a kid. I'm not buying it now."

"I never bought it," Ruth said as she stepped up next to her granddaughter. "Explain yourselves."

"Things have been tough financially for the business. We thought the new principal's salary would get us back on track, but that didn't happen. Then some changes in the school policies affected us. Basically, the dry cleaners is losing business."

"It's that new principal's fault," spat Ruth. "If the Board of Education hadn't brought in an outsider, you wouldn't be in this situation."

Justine put a hand on her grandmother's arm. "I know you're upset, but can you let Mom finish, please? I want to hear the facts, not your opinions."

Her daughter's response impressed Heather. The years of therapy were paying off. Heather didn't want to go into detail about their financial problems and embarrass either herself or Matthew, but their daughter deserved the truth.

"Your grandmother is partially right," said Matthew. "Not being a sports booster hurt us. Losing some key contracts didn't help."

"But my tuition is higher, so that played a part in it as well." Justine turned to her mom. "I can help. I'll pay for my tuition with the internship stipend."

Ruth's eyes bulged. "If you hadn't changed majors, this wouldn't be an issue."

"Mom, that's not the point." Heather slid her arm around Justine's waist and squeezed. "Justine is doing what is right for her. Teaching isn't her thing, and that's fine with us."

"Your father would be so disappointed in you."

Heather flinched under her mother's glare but was soothed when she felt Justine's arm slip around her.

Ruth turned her gaze to Matthew. "You're culpable for this as well. What husband can't support his wife?"

Matthew's face hardened. "It's a partnership, and we are both accountable for our actions."

Heather swallowed the bile that found its way to her mouth. "Mom, it's more complicated than just the tuition and the business. We had some unexpected bills. Selling the house is the quickest way to handle it."

"Which is where I come in," said Dot in her usual cheerful voice. "By the end of the week, the house will be under contract, and whatever issues are plaguing this lovely couple will be in the rearview mirror."

Ruth let out a puff of air that sent her ivory bangs flying. "Why did you choose this woman? Not only is she irritating, but there are so many better agents you could have picked."

Matthew held up a hand. "Ruth, there's no reason to be rude. If you don't like her, keep it to yourself. Otherwise, you're free to leave."

"Fine. Have it your way. This is a mistake, like so many others Heather's made in her life. You two fix it, because I will not be around to bail you out." Ruth stomped back to the house and slammed the door behind her.

Justine's gaze followed her grandmother. "Should I go talk to her?"

"It won't help, honey. She's upset with us. Anything you say is going to set her off," said Heather, as she turned to Dot. "I'm sorry about my mother. She's opinionated."

"I know. Everyone knows." Dot planted the sign in the front yard. "My job here is done. I'll be in touch." The agent smoothed her blonde hair into place, hopped back in her car, and sped off.

"That went well," Matthew mumbled.

"If you two would have told me what was going on, I could have helped," Justine murmured back.

Heather nodded. "You're right. But what's done is done, and now we need to move on."

"What are you going to do about Grandma?" Justine asked.

Matthew's jaw clenched, and he headed toward the house. "Drive her to the airport."

CHAPTER 22

"Once the house was on the market, it would be public knowledge," Matthew called out from the kitchen.

Heather eased onto the sofa, exhausted from her mother, cleaning, and sending Justine back to college. "But Dot let the cat out of the bag."

"At least they know. Although why you told them about the business is beyond me."

Heather mulled over his comment. She didn't feel good about spilling all the details, but she knew her mother. If Ruth sensed something was being kept from her, she would be like a fly at a picnic—annoying and unwilling to leave unless squashed.

"The end result is it cut her stay short. Win-win. But you've got to admit, Justine took it well. She surprised me."

"You told me she could handle the facts," Matthew said as he handed her a glass of pinot grigio before he plopped onto the couch with his beer. "You were right."

Heather took a long sip before she asked, "When was the last time you said that to me?"

"It's been a while. You were right about Angela, too, but

we're paying her back as soon as the house sells. First showing is Tuesday at one, and Dot scheduled the open house for Friday. She said no cooking past midnight tonight, so I thought I'd whip up a double batch of spaghetti sauce and a loaf of bread. Not sure when we will cook here again. Work for you?"

Heather pushed aside the wave of sadness she felt and stood up. She offered a hand to Matthew and pulled him off the couch. "Absolutely. I'll help."

They spent the evening in the kitchen, testing the sauce, making bread, and talking about what they would do once the bills were paid. The conversation started awkwardly, but they soon fell into an easy rhythm. Matthew tossed out some suggestions on improving the business at the cleaners, although neither of them were hopeful. Stadium loved its sports, and without a way to support the school, the dry cleaners couldn't compete with the other boosters.

"I could quit my job," Heather suggested. "Then the cleaners could get back into the booster club."

"You're under contract. If you do that, no one is going to hire you again. But maybe you start a side hustle—coaching kids on writing essays or something like that. If Shannon won't let you do it at school anymore, that would be a way to keep your hand in the game."

Heather pulled the bread from the oven while she considered Matthew's suggestion. Once the house was sold, the chickens would be gone too. She would have some free time on her hands. Helping the kids with college planning was supposed to be something the guidance department did, but that wasn't happening now. Shannon didn't prioritize it, so it had fallen by the wayside. No one was doing anything to draw Shannon's attention.

Heather laughed when she saw Matthew set the dining room table with disposable plates, forks, spoons, and cups.

"Glad you did this now and not when my mom was here. We wouldn't have heard the end of it."

"Since she's not here, let's make this easy. Neither of us wants to do dishes. I suspect we may not see your mother for a while."

They took the food to the table where they could serve themselves. On a whim, Heather grabbed a couple of candles they'd unearthed during their cleaning process and set them on the table. She lit them and stepped back. "Table's ready."

Matthew poured wine for each of them, then pulled out the chair for her. "After you."

Heather slid into the seat. She waited for Matthew before raising her wine. "I'd like to make a toast."

Her husband picked up his plastic cup.

"To new beginnings."

"To new beginnings," Matthew repeated.

They tapped their plastic cups together and sipped their wine. Heather looked at her husband, wondering if she should explain the meaning of her toast.

She wanted to start over with Matthew.

Heather took a bite of spaghetti as she thought about the self-work she needed to do. Her habits of telling half-truths and omitting details played a part in their marital issues. It might be time to put some distance between her and Brian. She had enjoyed spending time with Matthew the last few weeks. Her mother's visit aside, they worked well together.

She was chewing when Matthew said, "We should talk about where we're going when the house sells."

Heather's heart took off like a thoroughbred, and her body tingled from her hands to her feet. Matthew said *we*. She swallowed a squeal of delight, and a piece of pasta stuck in her throat. Heather coughed, freeing the food, but it took several minutes, a glass of water, and Matthew thumping her back before she was ready to speak.

"You want to stay together?" she asked with a croak, wishing she sounded more emotional than ill.

Matthew's brows drew down. "Yeah. What did you think we were going to do? Split up?"

She ducked her head to hide the tears that welled up in her eyes. Heather opened her mouth, but this time it was emotion, not spaghetti, that kept her from speaking. Instead, she nodded.

"Heather, we need to get better at communicating. Do I get frustrated with you? Absolutely. But you get upset with me, too. Life's too short. I married you for better or worse, richer or poorer, in sickness or in health. Your mom's taken care of the *worse*. We're experiencing *poorer*. Justine's issues and that choking episode hit *sickness*. We're covered."

He put his hand under her chin and lifted it. She gazed into his eyes, which sparkled for the first time in a long time. That light told her what she needed to know. They had hope.

"Let's figure out where we are going after the house sells, then we can get back to the *love and cherish* part."

She reached and traced his jawline, something she hadn't done in a long time. Matthew relaxed with her touch, and Heather placed a feather-light kiss where her fingers had been before she asked, "Does that mean the chickens can stay?"

Matthew chuckled as he took her hand and lifted it to his lips. "I guess that means we need to find a house to rent. But if that's what you want, let's make it happen."

CHAPTER 23

*H*eather jolted upright, her sweat-soaked pajamas plastered to her body. Her pounding heart felt like she'd been running uphill into a twenty-five-mile-an-hour headwind. She reached for her bedside alarm clock, her hand shaking. The LED display read 3:21 a.m. Why was she awake?

She fell back onto her pillow and stared at Matthew's empty side. She wanted him next to her, but they had agreed to meet with Dr. Austen before sharing a bedroom again. It would be a while.

Frustrated, Heather took deep, steadying breaths the way her therapist had recommended. The rhythmic pattern should have relaxed her. Instead, the smell of burning wood tickled her nostrils. Then the bitter aroma of burning plastic assaulted her. She knew why she was awake.

The house was on fire.

Heather jumped out of bed and ran to the door. It was cool to the touch, so she flung it open in time to see Matthew coming toward her from the guest room, his hair tussled and his chest bare. Her eyes stayed glued to Matthew's chest, realizing how much she missed him, before the smoke sent her into a coughing fit.

"You smelled it too?" he asked as he yanked on a T-shirt. "I'll go downstairs and see what's going on. It can't be too bad. The smoke detector hasn't gone off."

"You shouldn't—" Before she finished the sentence, the screeching blare of the smoke detector interrupted her, "say that!"

"Change of plans." Matthew took her arm, pulled her back into the bedroom, and closed the door. "Call 911 while I open the window and get the escape ladder set up. That's the quickest way out."

She grabbed her cell phone and dialed as she threw anything within arm's reach into her purse. It felt like an eternity before someone answered the phone.

"All lines are busy. Please try again."

"Damn it." Heather's heart sank as she shoved the phone into Matthew's hand. "How can an emergency line be busy?"

He slid the phone into his pocket and took hold of her arms. "Stay calm. Let's get out. Then we'll call again."

Matthew guided her out the window when she remembered: their wedding pictures; Justine's baby book; the last picture she took of her dad; Queenie; everything they owned. All of it would be gone if they didn't do something. She froze.

"What about the scrapbooks? The chickens? We can't leave them behind."

Matthew stared at her, one hand still holding her arm while the other steadied the escape ladder. "Those are replaceable. We aren't. Come on."

Heather scrambled back inside. "We have to go downstairs."

Without waiting for his answer, Heather dashed into the hallway. Smoke hung thickly near the ceiling. Brown particles swirled in the air, hitting her cheeks. She hunched and shuffled down the hallway, vaguely aware of the soft carpet beneath her feet.

Heather rushed for the stairs. But when her foot touched the first step, a searing pain radiated from her foot into her calf. She screamed as she jerked her foot up, but she lost her balance. Heather frantically grabbed for the handrail, but she missed it and tilted forward.

Her last thought was that it was stupid to die for a picture when something yanked her waist. Heather registered Matthew's arm hair scratching her skin in the space between her PJ top and bottoms before she shot backward. She stopped suddenly when she slammed into Matthew's chest, toppling them both to the floor.

"Do not run away from me again," Matthew muttered before he gingerly examined her bare foot. "Are you okay?"

"Yeah." Heather peered down the stairs and gasped at the sight of the smoldering carpet. In her concern about the scrapbooks, she had forgotten to put on shoes.

Matthew forced her fuzzy bedroom slippers into her hand. "Forget these?"

Heather slid on the slippers, wincing a little when the injured ball of her foot met the fabric. She gritted her teeth and focused on finding a clear path.

Matthew took her hand as they navigated down the stairs. They stepped over smoldering carpet, a missing tread, and the remains of a family portrait. Heather's stomach untwisted at the bottom of the stairs. The entryway was free of flames. Her relief was short-lived when flames shot out of the dining room. The scorched remains of her favorite blue drapes hung from metal rods that twisted from the fire's intensity. Blackened fabric rested on the seared oak floor next to the smoldering farm table, where she and Matthew had eaten a candlelit dinner only hours before.

She turned away from the sight as she stepped toward the living room, but Matthew's grip halted her progress.

"Heather!" Matthew yelled. "We have to get out of the house!"

She stared at Matthew's soot-streaked face and his panicked eyes. She struggled to free herself, but Matthew's grip tightened. An alarm blared over the crackling of the fire. Matthew pulled her toward the front door, but she twisted and broke free.

Before he could catch her, Heather launched herself into the living room.

The faux-leather sofa spewed an acrid plastic stench as it shriveled up like the Wicked Witch of the West after Dorothy threw a bucket of water on her. Heather's head spun when she inhaled the fumes, so she switched to shallow breaths. She stumbled to the bookshelf and yanked down scrapbooks as fast as she could.

An ominous crackle warned her it was time to go. She took Justine's senior photo album from the shelf and cradled it as she exited the room. Heather slowed at the doorway, wondering if she'd missed anything, when the chandelier plummeted. It shattered in front of the bookcase where she'd been standing. The sight sent a chill through her body, despite the intensity of the blaze.

When she passed through the hallway, she saw Matthew standing where she'd left him. He didn't speak, only ripped some books from her grasp, grabbed her arm, and didn't let go until they collapsed in the yard.

The sun peeked above the horizon as the last of the fire trucks drove away. Heather snorted at the irony of the situation. Sunrise, a time of rebirth and fresh beginnings, lit up the ruin of her damaged house.

The front door lay splintered into pieces. The porchlight dangled from loose electrical wires, swinging in front of the hole where the door used to be. Puddles of dirty water decorated what remained of the front porch. Smoke lingered in the air above trampled bushes and ravaged flower beds. A tattered flag that once proclaimed Stadium Football for the Win lay shriveled and withered from the fire's heat.

She closed her eyes and focused on her breathing. Heather looked on the positive side. She had gotten the scrapbooks out. Justine wasn't home. Matthew was safe, except for a few scratches. The chickens had survived. Everything was fine.

Except the house. The house that had been the answer to their financial problems was now a tangle of partially burned wood, missing shingles, and burnt plastic.

"You're shivering," Matthew said as he placed a blanket around her shoulders. "The girls are on their way."

Blinking back tears, Heather rested her head on Matthew's shoulder. "Thank you."

Matthew wrapped his arm around her shoulder, and they stood side by side for a few minutes. The chickens cawed, expressing their dismay at the turmoil. There would be no eggs for a while.

"The living room is gone, but the firefighter said structurally we should be okay," Matthew explained as he pointed to what remained of the house. Heather recognized the confident tone of his voice. "We'll postpone the sale while we rebuild. Or maybe demolish the house and sell the land. Have to see what insurance says."

The thought of demolishing the house scared her more than selling it. At least, if someone bought it, she could still drive by and see it. "Can we talk about that later? I need some time to process."

Stacey's SUV pulled into the drive, followed closely by Angela's sedan. The vehicles maneuvered around the debris in the driveway and parked short of the garage. The drivers' doors flung open in unison.

Tears streamed down Heather's face as Angela and Stacey rushed toward her. She threw off the blanket from her shoulders and ran into her friends' embraces.

"You're okay!" Stacey squeezed her arm. "That's all that matters."

Angela added, "It's only stuff. You can replace it."

They looked up at the sound of a horn. Rachel's car skidded to a halt in front of the house. Rachel popped her head out. "I would have been here sooner, but I had to pick up Chris."

The passenger's side door swung open, and Christine leapt out. She didn't wait for Rachel but sprinted across the yard and stopped right in front of Heather. "What can I do?" she asked, out of breath.

Rachel joined her friends and gaped at the house. "Wow. Did

your mother do this? I knew she was mad, but this seems a little excessive, even for her."

Angela took charge. "Rachel, knock it off." She waved toward Matthew, who was examining the remains of the front porch steps. "Heather, you and Matthew can stay with me until you get this sorted out. Your insurance company promised to send an adjuster first thing in the morning." She looked at her watch. "Which would be any time now."

"You talked to our insurance company? How'd you do that?"

"When Matthew called, I got the information. Don't worry about that now. Do you have clothes? Matthew said you made a pit stop in the living room for sentimental things—which was dangerous, in case you were wondering."

Heather pointed to her purse, hanging from the mailbox so it didn't get wet on the ground, and the scrapbooks that someone had placed in a large plastic bin. "That's it. I didn't grab much of anything. I could go in and get some clothes now."

"I've got stuff at Aunt Willa's you can use," Christine said. "The pants might be long on you, but it's something."

Stacey shook her head. "I'll stop at the store and grab some clothes and shoes for both of you. That way, you can get the right size."

Heather let the conversation wash over her while her friends planned and coordinated a relief effort. She and Matthew would have someplace to sleep, food to eat, and clothes to wear. The family scrapbooks were safe, and insurance work was underway. Everything was good.

Almost everything.

"What about the chickens?"

Angela's eyebrows rose. "Heather, I love you, but there is no way those chickens are coming to my house."

"Aunt Willa wouldn't allow that, either," Christine said, "unless you want chicken cacciatore for dinner tomorrow."

Stacey shook her head. "Sorry, not happening."

Heather turned to Rachel, who held up her hands in surrender. "My landlord would throw a fit, but I can call around and see who can help. Didn't you say Francine had mentioned taking them?"

"Her daughter."

Rachel pulled her phone from her pocket. "I'll stay here and make sure someone picks up the chickens. You and Matthew get settled."

After more hugs and chiding about risking their lives, the group dispersed. Christine rode with Stacey to the running store to put together the care package. They planned to drop it off at Angela's since she was leaving to get the guest room set up. Rachel headed down to the Poultry Palace to wait for Francine's daughter.

As Matthew pulled their car out of the drive, Heather stared at the remains of her house and wept.

CHAPTER 25

Two nights later, Heather slid into Angela's guest bed. The Egyptian cotton sheets enveloped her, soothing away some of her exhaustion and worries. The fire had disrupted their plans, but sharing a bed with Matthew was a positive side effect.

"You don't snore as much," she said to Matthew, who was setting his alarm. "What changed?"

Matthew shifted onto his back, his head resting on his arms. "I don't know. Maybe I'm happy to sleep next to you."

"Do you remember why you moved into the guest room in the first place?" Heather lay on her side so she could see him better. She frowned at the scabs on his arms and shivered at the reminders of the fire. She could have lost so much more.

"I couldn't sleep after we argued," Matthew said. He rolled over to face her. "I figured if I slept someplace else we couldn't fight. Looking back, it might have been better to talk about it than avoid it."

Heather nodded her agreement. The house fire had sparked a renewed connection between them, something they both acknowledged. They had work to do on their relationship, but this was progress.

"I made things harder." Matthew ran his finger on the back of her hand, sending tingles up Heather's arm. "I should have told you how I felt."

Her voice trembled. "I'm the one keeping things from you. We wouldn't be in this mess if it weren't for me."

"Sounds like dual culpability." His hand glided up Heather's arm and caressed her shoulder.

"It's actually shared accountability," Heather said.

Matthew raised an eyebrow.

"Sorry. Angela must be rubbing off on me."

"I'm purposefully ignoring that statement." Matthew shifted his body closer to hers. "I'm meeting with the insurance adjuster again in the morning. Can you join me?"

She shook her head, then added in a breathy voice, "Taking two days off put me behind."

"You could ask for more time off. A house fire is a major life event. Shannon would understand."

She lifted her hand and let her fingers slide through Matthew's hair. Heather missed stroking the soft locks. "Maybe. Considering our current situation, I can't afford to rock the boat."

Matthew took her hand and pulled her closer. "Fair enough. But promise me something."

A spark of anticipation ignited in her chest, and she licked her lips. "What?"

"Don't hide things from me. If this fire taught me something, it's that I don't want to lose you. I love you, Heather, and we will make this work."

Heather's pulse raced, and she felt her hands tremble. She couldn't remember the last time Matthew had spoken those words. She let them sink in, her stomach fluttering, and said in a shaky voice, "I love you too."

Matthew's lips pressed against hers, and those were the last words either of them spoke that evening.

* * *

LATER THAT WEEK, Heather gazed at Stadium High School's agricultural building and smiled. Sharing a room with Matthew again meant she got less sleep than usual. But Heather felt more energized and invigorated, not to mention more in tune with Matthew, than she had in years.

"For someone whose house burned down, you seem awfully chipper," said the FFA sponsor.

Heather forced herself to concentrate on the other teacher. "It could have been worse, I guess. Plus, I'm thankful you could take the chickens for me, Tina."

She followed the FFA sponsor to the poultry area. Francine's daughter couldn't take the hens on such short notice, but Rachel figured Queenie and her friends would be safe in the care of the students. Heather didn't know why she hadn't thought of that before. She could see her chickens whenever she wanted—or when she had time to make the walk from her office to the coop.

"This is a win-win for us. Shannon denied my request for eggs and a hatching lamp. And since I don't need those with full-grown chickens, the students will no longer miss out on the poultry unit. The chickens are welcome here until you get the house repaired. Did you find out what started the fire?"

"A romantic dinner by candlelight." Heather repeated what she told everyone who asked. "Never leave candles unattended. They are one of the leading causes of house fires." She ignored the nagging guilt she had felt since the fire investigator revealed the cause. Matthew swore he blew out the candles after dinner, but Heather chided herself for not double-checking.

Tina turned when she heard a student call out. She mumbled

an oath before saying, "Ms. Parker is heading this way. Who knew stilettos would make it to the barn?"

Tina and Heather watched Shannon navigate the dirt floor. The principal was out of place in the barn. Dirt coated the hem of her black pantsuit, and dust flew up into the air with each step. Halfway across the arena, the principal wobbled on the uneven ground before catching her balance.

"Serves her right if she fell on a cow patty," Tina said quietly so only Heather could hear. "The smell would never come out of that suit."

Heather pressed her lips together to keep from laughing. The situation wasn't funny as much as nerve-wracking. Heather hid her shaking hands in the pockets of her capris, but the last thing she wanted was to talk to the principal. Now that Shannon knew about her hiding spot, Heather needed someplace else to elude her boss—and quickly, judging from the expression on Shannon's face.

"Miss Harrison, it's been brought to my attention you have a recent addition in the barn. Mind if I ask where you got funding for it?"

Heather clenched her hands into fists and said, "The chickens are mine. I can't leave them at the house after the fire, and Tina is using them to fill the missing piece in the agricultural curriculum. No cost to the school."

Shannon glanced between Heather, Tina, and the chickens before nodding. "Miss Harrison, thanks for helping a fellow teacher. Can you give us a minute? I need to discuss some other matters with Mrs. Ramsey."

Tina blurted out, "No problem," at the same time she rushed across the arena.

Heather envied her coworker's ability to walk away from the principal, but wishful thinking wasn't going to help this morning.

"I'm headed back to the office if you want to talk there," Heather said.

"We can talk here." Shannon stepped closer to the coop. "How are you holding up with the house? You haven't taken much time off."

"No. Too much to do around here." Heather raised her index finger at the look Shannon gave her. "Digital textbook rollout is complete, and there have been minimal issues. Dress code adherence is up. Francine has embraced the attendance system, and I'm getting ready for the first truancy hearing. Everything is under control, considering the circumstances."

She expected a comeback from Shannon, but the principal continued to walk around the chicken coop. When she reached the opposite side from where Heather stood, Shannon said, "You raise chickens. I wouldn't have guessed."

Heather's curiosity piqued. "Something I enjoy in my free time."

"From what I can tell, you don't have much free time . . . which makes me feel a little guilty for what I'm about to ask next. Especially after your update. Let me start by saying you impress me. I didn't expect you to adapt to the situation as fast and efficiently as you have. Add in your personal circumstances, and I assumed you would want additional time off to deal with things."

Nervous energy flooded Heather's body. She couldn't wait to tell Matthew that she'd been right not to ask for any more days off. But something about Shannon's behavior seemed off. The principal didn't beat around the bush, and Shannon wanted something from her.

"What's going on?"

Shannon kept her eyes on Queenie, who stared back. "The school counselor missed college application deadlines. I've had several angry parents in my office—who did *not* have appointments." A resigned grin appeared on Shannon's face. "Which tells you how serious this is. I need you to step in and help fix things. Are you willing to do that?"

"Absolutely. It would be my pleasure." Heather struggled to remain calm when she felt like jumping up and down. Her enthusiasm fell a little when she wondered how she could fit the extra hours into her schedule, but, for the students, Heather would figure it out.

CHAPTER 26

"You shouldn't have agreed to help the school counselor."

Matthew held up a blackened book from a box of items the restoration specialists had saved from the wreckage. The insurance company had hired the specialists, but Heather wasn't sure it was worth it.

"Do you want a burnt copy of Kafka's *The Metamorphosis?*"

"That's Justine's copy from high school. She said to trash anything covered in soot . . . which are most things, it seems."

Spending Saturday night deciding what to keep and what to trash from the fire wasn't Heather's ideal evening, but it had to be done. The problem was that the pile didn't seem to get smaller.

"Was I supposed to tell Shannon no? I still have a shot at getting the principal position when she leaves. I need her recommendation."

"She's leaving?" Matthew asked.

Heather contemplated the question as she pried apart two books, which might have once been the first and second books in the Chronicles of Narnia series. When the front cover crumbled into dust in her hands, she pitched the entire mess into the trash pile.

"That's what teachers are saying. She's fixing everything this year. There won't be anything else for her to do. She'll be bored. Plus, she goes to Dallas most weekends. Why would she want to stay?"

"Stadium's a great place to live. Most of the time," Matthew amended, then waved a vinyl album that had been warped into the shape of a taco shell. "Do you think Justine wants this?"

Heather sat back on her heels. "If you ask me about everything in the box, we're never going to get through it. Make a judgment call and move on."

"The last time I did that, you yelled at me for getting rid of a damaged photo of your parents." Matthew tossed the album in the trash pile and continued scouring. "I'm confused about what's considered a keepsake and what's junk."

Heather swallowed her frustration as she recalled Dr. Austen's words of advice. When Justine's illness was at its worst, the therapist said, *"Conflict won't solve the problem. Both of you need to work through the grief this brought to the surface."* They weren't dealing with Justine's illness anymore, but the fire triggered pain.

Heather filled her lungs with a calming breath. "If it could be sold or used, keep it. If it has sentimental value, keep it. If it is beyond recognition, throw it away."

"What about the chicken coop?" Matthew asked.

Heather glanced toward the backyard, where the empty Poultry Palace stood, and sighed. The school didn't need the coop, and she couldn't take it to Angela's. "Might as well sell it."

"Thank you. Was that so hard?"

Heather bit her lip. She reminded herself that Matthew was under as much stress as she was—more if she considered that the town was avoiding the cleaners like the plague.

Heather turned her attention to a set of decorative vases that had survived the fire. She had hated them when her mother gave them to her as a wedding gift years ago, but she'd kept them. When she tossed them into the trash pile, a tension she didn't realize she carried released. She felt lighter, as if she could float away. Heather wondered if she would feel the same way about the Poultry Palace, but before she could decide, Matthew took her hand.

"I shouldn't be so snarky," he said. "Letting go of the coop is a big deal for you. I'm sorry."

She took in Matthew's face, smudged with soot, and let out a sigh of relief. "Thank you. That's nice to hear."

They stood there, holding hands, studying each other. Heather knew they were standing in the ruins of the house, but all she could see was her husband.

"Can I kiss you?"

"I don't know. Can you?" Rachel would have been proud of her.

Matthew chuckled, then leaned toward her. She smelled the coffee on his breath, as well as the sharp tang of his cologne. Their lips brushed, making Heather's tingle. She moved closer, deepening the kiss, but Brian's voice bellowed from the open front door. "Hello? Anyone home?"

Heather dropped her head onto Matthew's shoulder in disbelief.

"What is he doing here?" Matthew mumbled.

"I don't know, but we are about to find out." Heather stepped back and dusted off her clothes, which did nothing but smear soot down the front of her shirt. She called out, "Back here."

Brian strolled into the room carrying a bag and a cup carrier with three cups of steaming coffee. Heather saw the moment he registered the extent of the damage to the house. The smile fell from his face, and he halted. He spun around, taking in the entire scene.

"Wow. Just wow. You two are lucky to be alive."

"It wasn't that bad," said Matthew, "although we could have gotten out sooner if someone hadn't wanted to save scrapbooks."

"I didn't have copies. That's being remedied as we speak. What's up?" Heather asked.

Brian held out the bag and the coffee. "The teachers heard you were cleaning out this weekend and wanted to do something. I thought food would be good so you could spend more time working." He edged around a pile of soot that used to be a side chair and walked to the coffee table, which was still recognizable. "Here's coffee, a family portion of fried chicken, mashed potatoes and gravy, green beans, and biscuits, courtesy of my cousin's new restaurant in Glen Valley. And Betty made you an apple pie. It's still warm. This should be enough for a couple of nights."

The mention of chicken saddened Heather, but she knew they weren't hers. "Thank you. That was kind of everyone."

He placed the carrier and bag on the table and pulled an envelope out of the bag. "We also took a collection. Rachel said insurance is covering the repairs to the house, but you're responsible for replacing everything else." Brian tapped the envelope on his other hand. "This should get you a good start."

Matthew glared at Heather, who guessed their next private conversation would be about how much she discussed with her friends.

"We can't take that," he said. "Heather and I have it covered."

"From where I'm standing, you need all the help you can get. Take it. All the teachers donated. Well, everyone but Hollis, but that's to be expected. Man's as stingy as Scrooge." Brian looked around the room again. "Do you know how this happened?"

Heather ignored the question and said, "Matthew, why don't you take a break and eat? I'll be there in a couple minutes." She ignored the expression on her husband's face and mouthed,

"Please?" Matthew hesitated before he picked up the food and drinks and headed to the kitchen.

"Hey, Matthew," Brian called out.

Matthew stopped but didn't look back.

"My cousin needs a cleaner. If you're interested, call him. I put the number in with the cash."

Matthew's back stiffened, but he turned around and faced Brian. He uttered a curt thank you before continuing into the kitchen.

Brian picked up a blob of plastic that rested on the floor. "I always wondered what happened to TV remotes when they got hot." He set it on what remained of the coffee table. "I see Matthew still isn't a fan. You know, your husband is the only one in town who doesn't think I walk on water."

Heather didn't know whether she should be embarrassed by her husband's nonconformity or irritated by Brian's arrogance. She let it slide and said, "Thanks for bringing all this. I need to get back to work. Was there anything else?"

"I know you have a lot on your plate, but I have two requests."

Exhaustion had her sitting on the still-damp sofa. She saw Brian studying her out of the corner of her eye.

"You okay?"

"Tired. It's been a week. What do you need?"

Brian started to sit but changed his mind. He looked down at her instead. "First one is from football parents. The guidance counselor isn't helping students with college applications. I've got the athletic side of it taken care of, but could you step in on the academic side?"

"Shannon asked me to help. I'm setting up meeting times during lunch for students to meet with me. Get me the names of the players, and I'll add them to the list."

Brian picked soot off his shirt. "Yeah. Well. The thing is the guys can't meet during school. I told the parents you could do this after school hours." When Heather raised her eyebrows, Brian added, "They'll pay you. You don't have to do this for free."

Heather paused. Shannon hadn't offered extra pay. Heather might skate a fine line, but the extra money would help. Rather than commit herself, she said, "I'll have Angela check my contract to make sure I can do that. And I'm telling Matthew about it."

"Fair enough." Brian pulled another envelope from his pocket, which Heather immediately recognized. "Second favor. Can you drop this off at the superintendent's tomorrow? Between school and practice, I can't get over there during business hours. I don't feel good about leaving it in the drop box. It's better if you hand it to him directly."

Heather took the envelope but wondered if she should confess she had given the last envelope to Regina. Instead, she nodded. "Yeah. I can swing by."

"Great. I knew I could count on you." Brian clapped his hands, sending soot everywhere. "You should go eat dinner before it gets cold."

She walked Brian to the door and watched his Porsche pull out of their driveway. As the taillights faded, apprehension spread over Heather. Was it odd that Brian had figured out how to get her paid for helping students? And had Regina gotten the last report to the superintendent? She shook off those worries and focused on the one sitting in the kitchen. Matthew needed to know about helping the athletes. She hoped she could explain it without upsetting the new balance in their relationship.

CHAPTER 27

"I can't thank you again for everything you've done for us. Hosting Thanksgiving dinner for Justine and us was above and beyond, but we should get out of your way."

Heather looked around the room she and Matthew had shared for two months. So much had changed since the fire, but they still had a way to go.

Angela leaned against the doorframe. "You're welcome to stay for Christmas. I told Justine she could hang a stocking if she wanted."

"We appreciate it, but we're going to celebrate with Justine at school. She's got an intersession class plus her job, so she can't come back to Stadium for the holidays." Heather walked to the nightstand and checked the drawers again. "Matthew can't find his glasses. If you find them, let me know. I'll run by and pick them up."

"Can do," said Angela. "I miss you already, although I won't miss watching the two of you getting all cozy together. Makes me a little jealous. You shouldn't flaunt your marriage in front of a pathological single woman."

"Funny." Heather was glad Angela didn't know exactly how cozy they'd gotten in her guest room. "We're working things out."

"I heard. The walls are thin. I need to talk to a contractor about that."

Heather's cheeks got warm, and she threw a pillow at her friend.

Angela caught it and replaced it on the bed. "I'm happy for you. You and Matthew are good together. You had to figure out how, though."

"Well, we still need to figure out what to do with the dry cleaners. We hoped people would come back after the football season was over. Instead, we're getting blamed for Stadium's loss of the state championship. I told Shannon pink uniforms would be a problem."

Angela smoothed out some wrinkles on the guest bed before she returned the pillow to its place. "How's the college prep work going?"

"Great. I forgot how much I miss working directly with the students."

"You know, there's nothing stopping you from setting up a business on the side. If you expanded to the neighboring schools, you would put a dent in Justine's tuition. Maybe bridge the gap for the cleaning business."

Heather peered into the adjoining bathroom but still didn't find Matthew's glasses. "Yeah. Shannon's given me her blessing as well. It's a lot of work, though, on top of being the attendance czar and everything else."

"But you would have more income overall. You'd be flexible to make some other decisions. Depending on how things go, you could leave school and do college prep work full time."

The thought of answering to only herself sounded amazing, but Heather squashed the dream before it took hold. "I'd lose benefits. We need medical to cover Justine's therapy and meds."

"In a couple years, she'll have a job and her own health insurance. Think about it, Heather," Angela said. "You could be in control of your time and still work at the cleaners. Matthew could reduce his costs. Branching out to other schools means the cleaners would have a bigger market to draw from. No more attendance czar. Plus, it would get you out from under Brian."

Heather stiffened at Brian's name. "What's that supposed to mean?"

Angela straightened and transformed into her attorney persona right in front of her. "The girls and I wanted to say something, but we never found the right time. Rachel said Brian shows up at the oddest times, bringing you treats. The football players paid for your help with college applications when no one else did. You've been at the district office more often than usual."

The back of Heather's throat burned. It felt like Angela was building a case against her. "Are you spying on me?"

"Not intentionally. But people talk. Brian's up to something."

Heather looked away. Angela wasn't telling her anything she didn't know. But knowing it and being confronted with it were two different things.

"Please tell me you aren't getting your news from the gossip brigade. Those ladies have nothing else to do but speculate on everyone else's misfortunes."

"I'm going to ignore that." Angela folded her arms.

Heather felt like a student caught cheating on a test, but she refused to admit the truth. "You sound as paranoid as Matthew. Brian's trying to help. That's it."

"*I'm* trying to help. So are Rachel, Stacey, and Christine. You and Brian have a history. I get it. But watch out. If Brian drags you into something, you might not find a way out."

Rather than argue with Angela, Heather said, "If you want to help, a better way would be to figure out where to move the chicken coop. The school has their own coop, and the renovation crew said it's in the way. It could get damaged."

Angela's arms dropped to her sides. "Fine," she said in a chilly voice. "But don't say we didn't warn you."

CHAPTER 28

As she drove away from Angela's, Heather stewed about their conversation. Her friend loved her and was looking out for her best interests, but Angela was overreacting. Heather had done nothing out of the ordinary for Brian's players. Sure, she got paid, but that was allowed. And since when was it a crime to drop off an envelope for a coworker?

She didn't want to ruin the rest of her drive with these spiraling thoughts, so Heather switched on the radio for some distraction. Her favorite Christmas carol came on, and she sang at the top of her lungs. By the time the song finished, Heather's spirits were high.

Then the announcer came on. "Horton's Dry Cleaners sends this out to the Stadium High School football team: 'The three-peat state championship wasn't in the cards, but Horton's will be there for you next year.'"

Heather flicked off the radio and returned her attention to the road. She didn't need to focus, though. There was no one on the road, usually one joy of living in a small town. But right now, Heather wished she could vanish into a crowd. Everyone knew what she was doing and when. It was suffocating in a way. Why couldn't she do her job, live her life, and be left alone?

Her mother's ringtone filled the car, and Heather groaned. She'd been avoiding Ruth, not wanting to be guilted into spending the holidays with her mother. Not to mention the fire safety lectures were getting old. But if she didn't answer, Ruth would call back.

Heather clicked her hands-free device. "Hello, Mom."

"Did you get the fire blankets I sent you?"

Heather clutched the steering wheel, chiding herself for answering. Her mother had a one-track mind. "Yes. Thank you. That was considerate of you."

"It was."

Heather consciously relaxed her shoulders. Leave it to her mother to miss the sarcasm in her response.

"What's the cleanup status?" Ruth continued.

"The restoration team starts after New Years."

"How long will you be in the rental house?"

"Six months or so. They can't estimate it until they've assessed everything. The damage looks superficial, but if they get into the work and find something major . . ." Heather's voice drifted off. She didn't know what they would do if things were worse than expected.

"Do you need money?"

Heather frowned down at the screen, wondering what had gotten into her mother. Ruth never offered financial help.

The car drifted onto the shoulder of the road, making a loud rattling sound when it ran over the rumble strip. Heather forced her eyes back onto the road, swerving a bit to get back in her lane.

"What was that?"

"Nothing." Heather cleared her throat, wondering how to respond to her mother's question. The answer was yes, but that yes included strings that Heather knew she didn't want. Self-preservation seemed like the best route, so Heather said, "We're okay. Insurance is paying for most of the house stuff."

Heather stopped at the next intersection. No one was around, so she took a minute to rest her head on the steering wheel and regroup.

"All you have to do is ask. I'm more than willing to help."

Heather's hands shook, and she was glad no other cars were around. "Really? Because it didn't seem like it in October."

"I handled that poorly. I'm embarrassed to say that it took Justine's phone call for me to understand I had overstepped my bounds. I was wrong. I'm sorry. I'll do better in the future."

Heather sat back up in the driver's seat. Justine told Matthew she had called her grandmother, but their daughter hadn't shared what was said. Whatever transpired had made an impact.

She continued through the intersection and said, "Okay."

"In that vein, I want you to know that you and Matthew raised a mature and well-adjusted daughter. I may not like the fact that she doesn't want to be a teacher, but I admire her for going after what she wants. You need to be confident in yourself to do what other people view as the wrong decision. Which leads me to the next subject. Justine told me you're doing some college prep work with students after hours."

Heather braced herself for the criticism she knew was coming.

"I'm proud of you. Your father would be too."

Heather's mouth dropped open. She didn't know what to say, so she settled for, "Thank you."

Ruth laughed. "You sound skeptical."

"This wasn't what I expected when I answered the phone."

"Well, maybe you should expect more of me from now on. I'm here for you. I always have been. Okay. Enough confessions.

Mahjong starts in ten minutes, and I need to get ready. I am serious about helping. Let me know what I can do."

Ruth ended the call before Heather could respond. It didn't matter, though. Heather was speechless.

CHAPTER 29

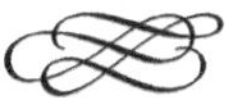

"I'm too old for this. Let's find another hobby aside from running," Rachel whined. "My feet hurt, and these shorts chafed my thighs."

Angela nodded. "She's being dramatic, but I'm still a little tipsy from New Year's Eve."

"That was a week ago. Today is the perfect day for a run!" Stacey raised her hands in the air. "We should enjoy it."

Heather assessed the gray sky and clouds. "It's going to rain, and we're going to get soaked. How is that gorgeous?"

"Any day you can get out and do whatever you want is a gorgeous day." Stacey turned to Angela, who snorted. "You have anything to add?"

"Honestly? I'm ready for coffee and a scone."

Heather threw her head back and laughed. She laughed so hard that tears streamed down her cheeks. Her friends stared at her, but she couldn't stop to explain what was so funny. Heather held up her index finger and waited while she calmed down and caught her breath.

"Sorry. I've waited years to hear Angela ask for a carb."

"She's got a point," Rachel said. "This is a rare occasion. If

Angela is asking for a scone, we should deliver. We are her friends, you know."

Stacey opened her mouth to protest as a torrent of rain fell from the sky. The four friends dashed for cover beneath the park's picnic shelter.

"That's one way to avoid running," Heather said.

"Let's wait here until it clears up," Stacey said, pulling out her phone and tapping it. "My weather app says it will stop in . . . crap—three hours."

"I don't have that kind of time"—Angela pulled her keys out of her jacket—"and now I have scones on the brain. Who wants to go to Betty's?"

Two hands flew into the air.

"Fine." Stacey pulled her hood over her head. "Let's go ruin months of exercise for five minutes of sugar."

* * *

"ADMIT IT! Five minutes of sugar is so much better than getting drenched." Rachel took a bite of her bear claw. Her eyes rolled back as she let out a soft groan. "So much better!"

Stacey sipped her coffee and picked at a blueberry muffin. "If we are going to blow off the training run, we still need to catch up on things. Heather, how's the rental house?"

With her mouth full of *pain au chocolat*, Heather gave a thumbs-up while she ate.

"It's quieter at my house now," Angela said with a smirk and an inappropriate gesture suggesting the reason behind the noise.

Heather winced as she swallowed the unchewed pastry left in her mouth. "Can you stop? It's embarrassing."

"Why? Because your marriage improved, and Angela got a front-row seat?" Rachel winked. "You've been in a much better mood at school, too. Even with all the extra work you've got. Which begs the question: what's your secret? Lingerie? Wine?"

Heather playfully nudged Rachel's arm before taking a sip of coffee. She refused to discuss her sex life right now.

"What's the extra work?" Stacey's voice lowered. "Did the principal assign you more stuff to do?"

Angela's lips pursed and her eyes narrowed, but Heather ignored her friend's irritation and turned to Stacey. "I got some of the college prep stuff back. If I play my cards right, when Shannon leaves at the end of the year, the board will see me as a team player and give me the principal position."

Three sets of eyes stared at her, and Heather squirmed in her seat.

Rachel leaned forward. "How do you know Shannon's leaving? Something tells me she isn't a one-and-done sort of principal."

Stacey patted Rachel's arm. "What she's trying to say is that nothing is guaranteed. You don't know what Shannon is going to do, so maybe don't get your hopes up."

"Have you thought about our conversation?" Angela asked.

When Heather gave a slight shake of her head, Angela turned back to Stacey and Rachel.

"She could start her own business. Offer post-high-school educational guidance. College prep and vocational counseling. Help in writing application essays and finding scholarship opportunities. The high school will never promote anything but four-year universities, so this fills a gap. Plus, she'd make more money and have more flexibility."

Rachel did a drumroll on the table with her hands. "That's a fantastic idea. I saw what you did for Sophia. She's in the running for several scholarships because of you. I'd refer my students to you in a heartbeat."

"I'll file your business documents and set up whatever intake forms you need." Angela took out her phone and started tapping away. "I'd need to do some research to figure out if an S corp or LLC is your best option."

"I appreciate it, but I need to keep my job. The dry cleaners is a mess. Two entrepreneurs in one family will not cut it. We've got bills to pay." Heather pursed her lips, then let out a sigh. "The extra money from the football parents is nice, but I can't branch out right now."

Her friends exchanged a look before fixing their gazes on her. She rolled her eyes and took a large bite of the pastry to keep from saying anything else.

"Why are the football parents paying you?" asked Stacey.

Rachel's eyes opened wide. "That's a step up from the coffees Brian usually bribes you with."

"It's not a bribe. I helped with college applications, and the players couldn't meet during the school day. I'm being compensated for my time." She held up a hand when Stacey's mouth opened. "My contract allows it."

Angela set her coffee cup aside. "Just because something is allowed doesn't mean you should do it."

"Why are you still helping him, Heather?" Stacey asked. "He may be the town hero, but we all know he isn't that great of a person."

"Did you put them up to this?" Heather glared at Angela.

The attorney leaned back and crossed her arms. "My position hasn't changed from before."

"Look, I appreciate your concern. And I know you have my best interests at heart. But Brian has nothing against me. We are all working toward the same goal."

Rachel opened her mouth, but Angela interrupted, "We want what is best for you. You might not believe us, but when it turns out we're right, I hope it's not too late."

Heather pushed the rest of her *pain au chocolat* away and stood up. "I've got to go. I need to figure out what to do with the Poultry Palace. The FFA can keep the chickens, but Shannon said no more coops. Our new landlord isn't a fan, either. He said it doesn't fit the neighborhood—too extravagant."

"It has a chandelier. It's a smidge extra." Rachel offered her a conciliatory smile, but Heather frowned.

"Whatever. It's for chickens, and it isn't hurting anyone. Just like Brian isn't hurting anyone. Geez. Sometimes I feel like this entire town is out to get me."

"Well, we're not. We want to help, which you won't let us do," said Stacey. "We'll be here if you need anything. That's what friends are for."

"Even if I don't need help?"

Angela shot right back, "Even if you don't *want* it."

CHAPTER 30

The conversation with her friends nagged her on the way back to the rental house. Brian didn't bribe her; he gave her gifts, just like the chicken statue her friends had presented to her when school started. Why couldn't they see the difference?

The pouring rain didn't help her spirits. By the time she pulled into the driveway, Heather's mood was as gray as the sky.

She got out of the car and hurried to the house, shivering as the cold water drenched her body. All she wanted was to take a hot shower and flop on the couch. Water sloshed in her shoes, and her pants stuck to her skin, so she veered to the covered side entry of the house. Heather stripped off her soaked clothing and hurried to the bathroom. As she closed the bathroom door, the doorbell rang.

"Matthew, can you get that?" Heather called out.

He didn't respond, and Heather realized his truck wasn't in the driveway. The doorbell rang again. As much as she wanted to ignore it, the insurance company couriered paperwork regularly, and they couldn't afford to miss a package. She shoved her arms into her bathrobe and wrapped her hair in a towel as she walked to the front door. The courier would not be seeing her at her best.

The bell pealed again.

"I'm coming. Hold on a minute."

When Heather glanced through the peephole, a chill ran through her. It wasn't an insistent delivery driver. It was Shannon. Heather shuddered. The last time a school official came to her house unannounced, it was to inform her that two students had made a poor decision and didn't live to see graduation.

Heather flung open the door. Shannon stood composed, a khaki raincoat protecting her clothes. Rubber galoshes covered her feet, and an oversized golf umbrella with the mascot of her previous high school kept her perfectly coifed hair in pristine condition.

"Shannon? Is everything all right?"

"We need to talk. I considered waiting until after winter break, but we can't wait. May I come in?"

Heather wanted to tell Shannon no, but it was clear something was wrong. She stepped aside to let Shannon in. Her boss closed the umbrella and propped it up outside the door before she entered. It occurred to Heather this was the first time she'd ever seen the woman without her trademark stilettos.

Heather tightened the belt of the bathrobe around her waist. "Sorry about my attire. We went running and got caught in the downpour."

"I'll make this quick," Shannon said. "Did you know Coach Glover is blackmailing referees?"

"He wouldn't do that," Heather said, but she could hear the doubt in her own voice and her friends' warnings from earlier.

"Before you defend him, let me explain a few things. And how you're involved. After I was hired, the Board of Education shared its belief that the previous principal gambled on the outcome of the football team."

Heather rubbed her chin. "Everyone gambles on the football

team. That's part of Stadium's culture. Mrs. Hunsinger bet her cranberry salad recipe this year."

"Not like this." Shannon smoothed an invisible wrinkle from her raincoat. "It appears Mr. Whittaker blackmailed football officials to favor Stadium so he could make six-figure wagers with Las Vegas bookies. Someone tipped off the board, and Whittaker resigned rather than being fired."

Heather stumbled to the sofa and fell onto it. Whittaker loved Stadium High and its students. She couldn't believe he would do something like that. A numbness like the one that had arrived when she heard about her father's death settled in Heather's chest.

"Why are you telling me this?"

"I don't believe it was Mr. Whittaker."

Heather trembled but forced herself to meet the principal's gaze. She asked in disbelief, "You think it was me?"

Shannon shrugged. "You were on my list. Right place. Right time. But I had no proof. I watched for anything suspicious coming through the high school. A few months ago, I was at the district offices when you delivered an envelope to the superintendent."

The hair on the back of Heather's neck stood up. "That was one of Coach Glover's reports."

"How many have you delivered?"

Heather shivered from a chill she hoped was left over from the rain and not the questions Shannon was asking.

"I don't know. Four or five this year."

Shannon's eyebrow arched. "This year? You've done this before?"

"I've dropped things off occasionally."

Shannon walked to the far side of the living room, her boots squeaking with each step. When Shannon turned around, Heather recognized the expression on her boss's face. Shannon was confident about something. "Those reports are how *Coach Glover* blackmailed referees. Not Mr. Whittaker. I'm still working through the logistics on how the reports got from the superintendent's office to the refs, but Brian is the source, and you were the first part of the delivery mechanism."

The towel on Heather's head slipped, but she was too shocked to catch it as it fell to the floor. Heather asked, "Why are you telling me this if you think I'm involved?"

"I admit, originally, I thought it was you." Shannon fidgeted with the belt on her raincoat. "But after seeing how much you care for the students, it doesn't add up. I'm also aware of your financial situation—"

Heather interrupted. "Does the whole town know?"

"The gossip brigade is quite effective. You undersold them," Shannon said with a rueful smile. "If you were benefitting from the bribes, you wouldn't be in this situation. Brian, however, has too much disposable income for a high school coach."

An image of Brian's shiny Porsche Cayenne popped into Heather's mind. She blinked away the thought. "Is the superintendent in on this?"

"Not sure," Shannon said. "Did you ever wonder why Brian didn't deliver his own reports or just use the school mail?"

"School mail gets lost sometimes, and he doesn't like the system."

"Or he needed someone else to divert suspicion." Shannon sat down in the chair across from Heather. "He pulled you into this. Do you understand the implications?"

Heather's hands shook as she digested Shannon's accusations. "Brian wouldn't do anything dishonest. He's competitive and wants to win. I've known him for years. He's harmless."

But as she uttered the words, Heather slumped forward. Shannon was right. It made sense. All the deliveries were before games, and Brian always gave her a deadline to deliver them. There was no other explanation.

Tears filled Heather's eyes as she asked, "What happens now?"

Shannon rubbed her hands together. "Now that I've confirmed you aren't involved, I have more details to gather. But I need your help."

A weight fell from Heather's shoulders. "What can I do?"

Before Shannon could answer, Matthew called out, "Hey, I'm home. Who's here?"

In a quiet voice, Shannon said, "Coach Glover trusts you. At some point, he'll ask you to deliver another package. Let me know when he does so we can implicate him. And do all of us a favor: tell your husband before he finds out from someone else. That damn gossip brigade has moles everywhere."

Matthew walked into the room, and Shannon stood. She nodded toward him and said, "Mr. Ramsey, I'm Shannon Parker, principal at the high school. I'm aware I am not your favorite person, but as I was telling your wife, I would like to help in this matter."

"What matter?"

"I'll let her explain." Shannon turned to Heather. "We'll talk soon. Think about what I've said."

Heather sat frozen in place while Matthew walked Shannon to the front door. When the door closed, Matthew rushed to her side.

"Are you okay? Did someone get hurt?" Matthew knelt in front of her, taking her hands in his. "Your fingers are freezing!"

With tears streaming down her face, Heather repeated what Shannon had told her. Matthew sat on the couch and hugged her while she cried.

"He used me. Everyone saw it but me."

Heather didn't know how long they sat there, but her tears dried up, and Matthew kissed her head. He asked, "Do you want me to call Angela? Sounds like we need some legal advice."

"Aren't you going to tell me how stupid I was for believing

Brian? That I should have known better? That this is all my fault?"

Matthew's grip around her tightened. "It isn't your fault. Brian took advantage of you. Someday, I'll remind you that I told you he was up to something. But with everything going on, I am not blaming this on anyone but him. Heather, I love you, and we will work this out. For now, we need to get Angela's advice. Do you want to call, or do you want me to do it?"

"I'll do it. I made the mess, so I should take care of it."

Her husband stiffened at her words.

"What?"

Matthew let out a long sigh. "This is not great timing, but I should tell you where I've been."

For the first time since he came in the door, Heather realized her husband was as wet as she'd been.

"What's going on?"

"A customer came into the cleaners, and we got to talking. She needed a chicken coop."

Heather's heart sank. "Not today."

"You said you were ready to sell it. She offered a thousand dollars when I told her about the bells and whistles. You didn't answer the texts I sent, and I didn't want to miss the opportunity. I loaded it up and delivered it to her."

Heather dropped her head to her chest, but she found she was out of tears. Her father's creation was gone. Matthew had done what he thought was best. The only good thing about it was they had cash for Angela's retainer.

CHAPTER 31

"**I** still can't believe you're helping Shannon investigate Brian's bribery schemes," Rachel said. She propped up her feet on Heather's desk. "And that you didn't yell at Matthew when he sold the coop. Who knew your marriage would get stronger while your professional career crumbled?"

"Always the optimist, aren't you?" Heather motioned with her hand that Rachel should remove her feet. "What was I supposed to do?"

Rachel's shoes clunked on the ground, and she stretched out in the chair. "Exactly what Angela told you to do: keep your eyes open for anything that will help Shannon. That's the benefit of having a friend who is a lawyer and who has favors to call in. Also, for the record, we are not supposed to be talking about this."

"I'm aware. But it's been almost a month, and nothing's happened. Brian's avoiding me. He knows something's up."

Rachel took a mint from the ceramic chicken-shaped bowl on Heather's desk. As she unwrapped it, she said, "Relax. Brian's avoiding everyone. The buzz in the teacher's workroom is that he's still upset about the loss of the state championship. Even Mr. Hollis noticed, and that man is as blind as a bat—and, yes, the science department told me several times that bats are not blind. When do you think the house repairs will be finished?"

Heather took a mint as well, but instead of opening the package, she passed it from hand to hand. "Your guess is as good as mine. Every time the county comes out to inspect, something else gets flagged. First, it was faulty electrical. Then, the drainage needed to be cleaned out and some of it repaired. Last I heard, there is a plumbing issue."

"You never had plumbing issues."

"Have a fifty-thousand-pound fire truck drive over your water supply line and see what happens."

Rachel slurped on her mint. "Another reason to be a renter."

Someone knocked on Heather's door, and Rachel stood. "I didn't know you had an appointment. I'll get out of your hair."

Heather shook her head. "I don't. Just ignore it."

"You're becoming quite a rebel. Has anyone told you that?" Rachel gave her two thumbs up. "I approve."

The knocking got louder, and Brian's voice drifted through the door. "I can hear you in there. Can I come in? Please?"

Heather hoped she didn't look as panicked as Rachel did. Her friend leaned forward and whispered, "Remember what Angela said. Don't tell him anything. Pretend everything is normal."

"Easier said than done," Heather whispered back before calling out, "Come in."

The door swung open, and the scent of chocolate entered the office before Brian did. "Hello, ladies. I thought I'd find you both here." He set the coffee carrier on Heather's desk and pulled out a cup. He offered it to Rachel. "Hot chocolate? There are marshmallows and whipped cream on it."

"You had me at hot chocolate." Rachel took the cup and

settled in her chair. "Haven't seen you around much. That loss must have been rough."

The vein on Brian's right temple bulged. "Yeah. Not one of my finest moments." He handed the second cup to Heather. "Only whipped cream on yours. I remember your opinion about marshmallows."

"Ghostbusters blew that treat for me," Heather admitted when she took the cup. "Rachel and I are in the middle of a meeting. Did you need something, or is this just a chocolate run?"

Brian reached into his pocket and pulled out a business card. He handed it to Heather. "Give Jerry a call. He'll hook you up."

"Thank you." Heather glanced at the card and blinked when she recognized the name of the high end-furniture store in Dallas. "We can't afford anything right now, but I appreciate it."

"He owes me. Whatever you need, let him know. He'll work with you." Brian leaned forward as he removed his own cup from the carrier and tossed it into the trash. He started to the door, then paused and turned. "Hey, Rach, do you think I could chat with Heather for a few minutes? I need some advice."

Heather looked at Rachel. Maybe this was her chance to get the information Shannon needed.

Before she could come up with an answer, though, Rachel said, "I don't mind staying. Maybe I can offer some suggestions, too."

The vein in Brian's temple bulged again. "The player wouldn't appreciate it if they knew their English teacher sat in on the discussion."

Rachel settled back into her chair. "If this is a gripe session about me, I'm definitely staying."

Heather flinched when Brian's mouth opened, but his belly laugh confused her.

"You are a firecracker, aren't ya? This is nothing like that. I've got a student having some issues like Justine. I could use

Heather's perspective. No one's complaining about you, as far as I know."

Rachel shot Heather a look. Her friend was going to let her decide. Heather was nervous to be alone with Brian, but this is what she needed. Plus, Brian would get suspicious if she wasn't willing to help a student. When Heather was sure Brian was looking at Rachel, Heather nodded slightly.

"Brian, thanks for the hot chocolate. And Heather? Remember what Angela said," said Rachel. She stood up and left the office.

Heather licked her lips, hoping her face didn't reveal her trepidation. "I remember," she called out, her voice drifting into the hallway through the door Rachel left ajar.

Brian pushed the door shut before he sat down in the chair Rachel had vacated. "Sorry to do that, but you and I need to chat, Sugar."

"No problem." Heather picked up her cup to keep her hands from fidgeting. "Who's the student, and what's happening?"

Brian stared down at his feet, his next words muffled. "There isn't a student. I heard some news that affects you. I wanted to be the one to tell you."

Heather's heart raced. She had to look surprised when Brian told her he was blackmailing football officials. But now she would find out what was really going on, and things could go back to normal. Or as normal as possible.

Heather swallowed her relief and asked, "What is it?"

Brian's chest puffed out as he looked Heather in the eye. "The Board of Education extended Shannon's contract."

Heather didn't have to fake her reaction. Her grip on the cup loosened, and it slid through her fingers. She caught it before it hit her leg, but the hot drink sloshed onto her pants. "Ouch! That's hot." Heather opened her top drawer and pulled out some napkins. She dabbed at the liquid on her pants and assessed her thoughts.

Despite the minor pain in her leg and the large stain on her pants, Heather's shoulders lightened. She and Matthew still had an income issue, but Heather now knew her fate. Maybe she should follow through on a business of her own. Working for someone else was fine, but if she had no chance for advancement, now might be the time to jump ship . . . if Brian was telling the truth.

"You didn't know?"

Brian's question interrupted her thoughts. Angela recommended she act like everything was normal, so that's what she would do.

"No. It makes sense, though. She's doing a great job. And she's more assertive than Whittaker ever was." Heather stopped herself. The last thing she should do right now was bring up the former principal. She added, "Or than I ever could be."

She waited for Brian to contradict her, but he nodded instead. "You do what's good for the school and the students. Shannon likes to dig around in places she doesn't belong. Which is something else I want to talk to you about."

Heather didn't trust herself to hold the hot chocolate, so she put the cup on the desk. She folded her hands in her lap and waited.

"This is going to sound crazy, but hear me out. Shannon is out to get me. Ever since we lost state, she's been popping up in weird places, like the training room. Now the board's asking me a bunch of questions. Shannon's behind it. That's where you can help."

"Me?" The word came out at a higher pitch than she planned. Heather cleared her throat before continuing. "What can I do?"

"Mrs. Hunsinger saw Shannon's car at your rental last month. What was she doing there?"

She'd been so blown away by the principal's visit that Heather hadn't considered that someone else might have noticed. Heather said the first thing that popped into her head: "Shannon ran in Dallas. She saw the girls and me running a trail and stopped by to ask if she could join us." Heather doubted anyone in stilettos would enjoy running, but that was a problem for another day. "I don't know if that is friendship or desperation. I mean, what else is she supposed to do in Stadium? There aren't a ton of things to do around here."

Brian kept his eyes on her for longer than Heather thought was necessary before he said, "She's comfortable around you, which would make it easy for you to throw in a good word or two about me. The woman has more pull with the board than I thought."

"What exactly does the board think you did? Lose the championship on purpose?" She was joking, but Brian's head jerked, and Heather saw the fire light up Brian's eyes before he looked down. "That's what they think?"

When Brian looked up, his baby-blue eyes turned to ice. "Shannon is poisoning my reputation, and I need you to talk to her."

"Won't she think something is off if I suddenly start telling her what a great guy you are?"

"This type of thing requires something a bit more subtle. Next time she asks about truancy issues, let her know none of my players is a problem. I've adopted the digital textbook policy without a complaint." He pushed back his chair and stood up. "It is the least you could do for me. I'm pushing business to the cleaners, and I got you a deal on furniture. Although it would be easy to call Jerry and tell him you aren't interested."

That's when Heather knew. Matthew and her friends were right: Brian wasn't her friend. He used her, and she let him. A wave of anger grew in her chest, but she fought it back. She would act like her usual self, not like someone who finally understood how she'd been taken advantage of.

"I'll see what I can do." She made a big deal of checking her calendar. "I have a meeting with Shannon on Wednesday. I'll try to work something in then."

When Brian stood up, the bulging vein in his forehead was gone and his usual shining smile was back. "Thank you, Sugar! I knew I could count on you." He pulled an envelope from his pocket and tossed it on her desk. "That needs to get to the superintendent by the end of the day." Brian winked, then swaggered out the door.

Heather stood up and closed the door. She fell back against it and sank to the floor. She sat there, wondering what bothered her the most—that Shannon hadn't told her about her renewed contract, or that the principal was right about Brian. He didn't take her seriously, something that was obvious every time he called her Sugar.

As her breathing settled down, she decided it didn't matter. Brian had handed her what she needed to prove her innocence. She took a deep breath and opened the envelope.

CHAPTER 32

"This isn't smart," Angela said. "If Brian hears I'm part of this meeting, he'll know something's going on. He was suspicious as it was. What if Hunsinger drives by again?"

After Brian's ambush in her office, Heather wanted someplace Brian couldn't interrupt. She also wanted Angela present to witness whatever happened when she reported to Shannon. Moving the meeting to her house made sense, especially since she also needed to meet with the contractor.

"Christine is doing me a favor. She got Mrs. Hunsinger and the rest of the gossip brigade to help with a project at the Retirement Resort. Even if someone passes by, they won't know whose car is whose. The construction crew is from out of town, and it's the perfect place to meet with no one recognizing us. Just don't run up against anything. There's still soot and dirt everywhere."

Angela took a step away from the wall. "It's nice to have Chris back in town, although I don't see her much."

"That's because you're working all the time." Shannon's car pulled up, and Heather nudged Angela. "Game time."

Angela rolled her eyes. "You watch too many movies."

The three women met in the garage, which had sustained minimal fire damage and was the cleanest space in the house.

After Heather introduced Angela and Shannon, the principal eyed the space suspiciously. "Isn't your only daughter in college?" She pointed at one wall where four children's bikes hung. "What's with the retrospective on bicycles?"

Angela grinned and elbowed Heather. "She's got a good sense of humor. You didn't tell me that."

Shannon's face remained expressionless. "I'm the life of the party when I'm not cleaning up messes."

"Sounds like my lot in life." Angela nodded her agreement.

If it were a different situation, Heather thought her friend and her boss would hit it off. But it wasn't, and she needed to keep the goal of today's meeting front and center.

"I didn't want to get rid of them, so Matthew used them as wall art."

"Heather has a hard time with change. Not sure if you've noticed." Angela pulled a stack of papers out of her briefcase. "For the record, I'm here with Heather as her attorney. Not my choice of venue, but we needed to speak with you without Mr. Glover interrupting. He has that knack."

"I've noticed." Shannon dusted off a workbench and leaned against it. "What did you want to tell me?"

Heather looked at Angela, who nodded. They'd practiced what Heather should say.

"Brian showed up in my office earlier this week. He believes you are ruining his reputation with the board. Today's meeting is supposed to be an opportunity for me to convince you otherwise."

Shannon crossed her arms. "Before you continue, you might want to know that I signed my contract for next year. Even if you help with this investigation, you won't be the principal. The board also is having second thoughts on renewing your contract as vice principal. They think you're too close to Brian. Show me something to save your job. You're good at it."

Although Angela had warned her this was something the board could do, Heather's gut clenched. She wondered if Brian would care when he found out or if he was focused on saving himself.

Angela pulled an envelope from her briefcase and handed it to Heather.

Shannon's head cocked to the side. "What's that?"

"Proof that I'm not involved."

Heather handed it to Shannon, who opened it and scanned the letter inside. Shannon's eyes widened, and Heather knew Shannon understood she was reading evidence of Brian's blackmail attempts. This one was directed toward the head football referee. If the referee didn't promise to work the first game of next season and favor Stadium with his calls, Brian threatened to release some incriminating pictures he possessed of the referee and a woman—a woman who was not the referee's wife.

"How did you get this?" Shannon asked, a broad smile covering her face.

"He gave it to me on Monday and asked me to deliver it." Heather swallowed the pain in the back of her throat that had been there since she discovered what the envelope contained. She didn't understand why Brian still trusted her. She didn't care. This letter exonerated her. "I made copies before I dropped off the original with the superintendent."

"I don't understand why he's still bribing football officials," Angela said. "It's the offseason. Stadium lost its standing. Even if the refs are on Stadium's side, there's nothing that can be done until the fall."

Shannon folded the sheet of paper and slid it back into the envelope before speaking. "I can prove he threw the championship game this year. Can I keep this? It will build the board's case and help you keep your job."

Heather's lips parted, but nothing came out. Her glance flew to Angela, who answered for her. "What next?"

Shannon put the envelope in her purse. As she slung the strap over her shoulder, she said, "Brian will be suspended once we complete the investigation. Provided we have enough evidence, he'll be fired. The district will have to hire a new superintendent. And a new coach. It will be a PR nightmare." The sliver of a smile peeped out on her face. "I will be busy for years to come."

The humor in her voice made Heather remember something. "I told Brian you asked to join our running club. Not sure if you run, but you are welcome to join us."

Shannon opened her mouth, touched her tongue to her teeth, and closed it.

Heather frowned. "If you don't want to, that's okay. It was the first thing I thought of when he asked me why your car was at the rental, but if you don't—"

Shannon interrupted, "I'd love to. The treadmill is boring."

Angela and Shannon exchanged contact information and made plans for Angela to meet with the Board of Education's attorney as soon as possible.

Heather walked Shannon out the door. When she turned back to Angela, she couldn't stop shaking.

"That worked, right?" she asked Angela. "I mean, it felt good, but I don't know if it covered all the legal bases."

"You know that, as your attorney, I can't speculate."

"As my friend?" Heather held her breath for Angela's reply.

"You're going to be okay."

CHAPTER 33

Heather went through her mental checklist. Tonight's dinner needed to be perfect, so she made Matthew's favorites. Plated Caesar salads chilled in the fridge. Marinara sauce simmered, and water for the spaghetti boiled on the stove. Tiramisu from Betty's Coffee Bar rested on the counter. Candles would make the table look more welcoming, but under the circumstances, Heather decided against them.

She exhaled slowly, steadying herself. All that was left was to ask for Matthew's support. Shannon and the school needed her help to bring down Brian. There was too much at stake to do this without Matthew's blessing, since the dry cleaners could be ruined if the plan backfired. And she had finally learned that honesty was essential in a strong marriage.

The back door opened, then slammed. Matthew stepped into the kitchen and sniffed the air. His face beamed. "Garlic, basil, and oregano. You made marinara for dinner."

She draped her arms around his shoulders. "I made marinara for you."

"Well, thank you!" He wrapped his arms around her waist and drew her closer.

Heather melted into her husband's grasp. She raised her face to his, and her body relaxed as their lips touched. The kiss sent a tingling sensation from her head to her toes. At the blare of the kitchen timer, Heather reluctantly moved away from her husband. "Dinner's ready."

Matthew's mouth pressed over hers one more time before he squeezed Heather's arms. "Can I help with anything? I'd offer to light some candles, but we both know how that turned out."

"You can pour us each a glass of wine."

"On it." Matthew took the opened bottle of merlot and filled the glasses as Heather removed the salads from the fridge and placed them on the table. "Any particular reason for this lovely dinner?"

Heather pulled out her chair, but Matthew intervened. She smiled at him as she sat down. "Thank you. This is a moving-forward meal."

"If it gets me a homemade Caesar salad, I'm game." He noticed an envelope next to his plate as he picked up his fork and speared some romaine. "What's that?"

"My contract. Angela reviewed it. I got COLA plus five percent. Thanks to Deborah, the board knows I had nothing to do with Brian's scheme."

"I knew there was a reason she's my favorite school board member. I should offer her a discount on dry cleaning."

They ate in companionable silence for a few minutes. Heather didn't want to spoil the mood, but Matthew needed to know the rest of the story. She took a sip of her wine.

"Whittaker admitted why he resigned last year."

"Which was?" asked Matthew, his mouth full of food.

Heather moved the lettuce around on her plate. "Whittaker found out Brian was blackmailing referees and confronted him. Brian threatened to tell everyone about Whittaker's DUIs."

Matthew's fork stopped midway to his mouth. "Whittaker doesn't drink."

"Not anymore." Heather rested her hands on the table. "The DUIs were expunged years ago. Whittaker doesn't know how Brian found out. But when Brian threatened him, Whittaker didn't think he had a choice. He quit, making it look like he was the guilty party in the blackmail all along. That worked in Brian's favor."

Matthew put his fork on his plate and leaned toward Heather. He took her hand and squeezed it. "Brian planned to manipulate you like he did Whittaker, didn't he?

She swallowed the lump in her throat. "It might have worked if Shannon hadn't gotten the job."

"I guess we can be grateful for that," he said as he kissed her hand. When he looked back up at her, Matthew frowned. "What about the superintendent? Regina said he was acting weird."

The touch of Matthew's hand loosened the knot in Heather's stomach. "In a completely unrelated turn of events, he's interviewing for a job in Houston that he didn't want anyone to know about. He didn't know that someone on the cleaning crew was picking up the letters from his office and delivering them to the referees."

Matthew picked up his fork again and speared the last of his salad. "Somebody needs to vet their employees better."

"Yes, but Brian's persuasive. Always has been." Heather ignored the shame she felt. "He's good at convincing people to do what he wants them to do."

"Hmm."

Matthew put the last bite of salad in his mouth. Heather watched her husband chew, preparing for whatever questions he had.

"What happens next?" he asked.

Heather picked up the salad plates and put them in the sink. Her hands shook as she dished out hearty servings of the pasta and vegetables. She knew this was the right thing to do, so Heather cleared her throat.

"That's where I come in. Shannon and the board need me to get Brian to admit who else was involved and profiting from the fixed games. With that on record, the county sheriff can step in. But I'm not going to unless you're okay with it. If something goes wrong, it could destroy your business."

"You could be hurt." Matthew joined her at the stove, took the plates out of her hands, and put them on the table. "Brian isn't going down without a fight."

"The sheriff will be there. Shannon will be there. Angela's seen the plan, too. I'll be fine."

But Heather couldn't help but be frustrated with herself. She should have known she was only a tool Brian used to get what he wanted. He had no concern for anyone, which was something Matthew and her friends had known all along.

"I'm sorry. If I had listened to you, we wouldn't be in this situation."

Matthew shook his head as he beckoned her toward him. Heather relaxed into her husband's embrace and placed her head on his shoulder. His chest rumbled as he said, "No. We both made mistakes. And learned from them. In the future, you and I will be better at communicating, so you don't have to be bait for law enforcement."

Heather chuckled as she looked up at Matthew. "You're okay with this?"

"It needs to happen, and you're the best person to do it." They sat down and started eating dinner. After a few minutes, Matthew said, "I talked to Angela."

Heather's eyes widened. "What did you two talk about?"

"I told her it was okay for her to pay Justine's tuition—*if* she lets us pay her back. It's also time to have a conversation with Justine, letting her know you and I are on the same page. No more hiding things. You and I are an open book now."

Tears filled Heather's eyes, and emotion squeezed at her throat. She hadn't known it, but she craved Matthew's reassurance. Now that she had it, she was ready to ask her husband one last thing.

"What would you think if I didn't sign my school contract and started my own business? The girls think the college prep services I've been offering can be monetized. Maybe make more than I am now. And it's something I enjoy."

Matthew's brows furrowed as he chewed. He swallowed before he said, "It scares me, if I'm being honest. The dry cleaners is still struggling, although, if you didn't work for the school, I could be a booster again. That might draw back some customers."

Heather picked up the dinner plates and took them to the sink. "The gossip brigade will have plenty to say about Brian, and the dry cleaners is a logical place for that, especially since I was involved." She rinsed the plates. "But this mess makes me worry that if I don't take a chance, it might be taken from me. I've been living in the past, and now it's time to look ahead. Like Justine did. She knew teaching wasn't for her. I love working with students, but I want to do it on my own terms."

"It will be long hours and lots of work," Matthew said as he loaded the dishwasher, "but let's get your business up and running."

Heather stood at the sink watching Matthew clean up. His words sank in. He supported her and trusted her. They had more work to do, but this new chapter of their lives was just beginning.

She took a fork out of his hand and put it back into the sink before taking his hand. "We can do the dishes later. We have some unfinished business to resolve."

Matthew's nostrils flared. "I would have loaded the dish-washer sooner if this was the reception I'd get."

As she led him toward the bedroom, Heather shook her head. "It was actually your belief in me, but I wanted to finish my dinner before we had dessert."

CHAPTER 34

"Don't be nervous," Shannon said. "The sheriff wired your office and is close by in case anything happens. Get Coach Glover to admit he fixed the football games so he could bet on them. The more detail you can get, the better. That's it."

Heather's mouth felt like the Sahara Desert. She swallowed, but her saliva felt like sand, scraping down her throat, and she choked. Heather took a swig of water from the bottle on her desk. It took care of the dryness, but not the boiling anxiety in her stomach.

"I practiced this with Matthew."

He supported her decision to help the school district deal with Brian, but she was nervous. Brian wasn't the person she had thought he was, and she didn't know how this meeting would go.

"Your husband is more sympathetic than Glover will be." Shannon put her hand on Heather's and squeezed. "You can do this."

Heather ignored the tears that pricked at her eyes and nodded. "It feels weird, like I'm a spy or something."

"Consider it an appropriate response to Coach Glover's actions." Shannon sat down in the chair and crossed her legs.

Heather jittered from nerves. She needed a distraction. She stared at the principal's ever-present stilettos. "Those heels can't be comfortable. Why don't you wear flats or loafers?"

"You get used to them . . . although the new running shoes I bought from Stacey are heaven compared to my heels."

"She knows her stuff. She's the one who plans our running route. Hope you are up for a challenge."

"Why do you think I accepted this position?" asked Shannon.

Heather drummed her fingers on her desk, wondering if she should admit she knew the truth about Shannon's ex-husband and his fiancée. As far as Heather knew, no one outside of the running group knew the full story, not even the gossip brigade, which seemed impossible.

She tested the waters. "Lots of rumors, but the gossip in the teachers' lounge is inconclusive. Care to share?"

Shannon's gaze drifted to the window. The silence stretched out long enough that Heather didn't think she was going to respond. But she finally said, "Maybe someday. But I will say that everyone needs a change at some point in life. It was my time."

Heather raised her hand to her chest and grinned. This unwanted change in her life had helped her in ways Heather couldn't imagine. Shannon's arrival might have caused problems, but it sent Heather and Matthew on the path of reconciliation.

Heather jolted at the knock on the door, and Shannon stood up.

"It's time. Get him talking, and this will be over before you know it."

The knock sounded again, and Shannon opened the door. If Heather hadn't been paying attention, she would have missed the scowl on Brian's face when he saw Shannon. It vanished as soon as he entered her office, making a big deal of balancing the coffees on the tray he was holding while he checked his watch. "Heather and I have an appointment. Am I early?"

Shannon straightened, leveling her eyes with his. "We're finished." The principal walked out the door and closed it without a goodbye.

"Guess I should have gotten here sooner to save you from her wrath. What's wrong now, Sugar?"

Brian placed the tray on Heather's desk before handing her a cup. She recognized the offer as the bribe it really was and set it aside on the desk without comment. Brian raised his eyebrows as he dropped into the chair Shannon had vacated.

"Not thirsty?"

"I'll let it cool off," Heather said, ignoring the scent of the freshly brewed macchiato.

Brian propped his ankle on his knee, shifted an arm over the back of the chair, and leaned back. It reminded her of a king surveying his realm.

"Man, she must have dumped a heap of paperwork on you for you to let caffeine sit untouched."

"Something like that."

Heather's hands shook as she picked up a pen from her desk. She noticed Brian watching her, so she set down the pen and folded her hands in her lap. She rubbed her thumbs against her forefinger and met Brian's gaze. His baby-blue eyes appeared warm and welcoming as they returned her stare.

It was now or never.

"What did you ask me to deliver to the superintendent?"

Without hesitation, Brian said, "Reports. Like I told you."

Her stomach clenched. Brian, the man she thought she knew all these years, had blatantly used her.

She steeled herself. "Those weren't reports."

Brian's eyes narrowed, still warm, but filled with confusion. "Really? How would you know?"

She took a deep breath and returned his gaze. "I did what I had to do."

Brian blinked several times before his head fell back, and he belly-laughed.

Heather froze, confused by Brian's reaction. She expected denials, yelling, and threats, not amusement. She waited for his howling to die down, wondering how she'd missed this side of Brian.

When his amusement subsided, Brian brushed away the tears from the corners of his eyes and leaned forward to rest his forearms on Heather's desk.

"You have no idea how much I needed that. When have you ever done anything that someone didn't tell you to do? You are so predictable, which is why you would have made the best principal ever." The smile morphed into a sneer. "But now I'm stuck with Parker and those blasted heels."

Heather gripped the underside of her desk to keep from flinching. "Your players adore you. Why would you fix the games?"

Brian's eyebrows dipped low on his head as he leaned forward on her desk. His face was only a few inches from hers, and she could smell coffee on his breath. She half expected him to say he didn't know what she was talking about, but he shook his head.

"If you figured out this much, you come up with the rest."

She held her breath. If Brian didn't confirm what he'd done, Shannon wouldn't get the information she needed. Forcing herself to relax back in her chair, Heather remembered what she and Matthew practiced.

"For the money."

"We're paid next to nothing at this school. Hell, you tried to sell your house to make ends meet. How am I supposed to afford a decent lifestyle on a coach's salary? My Cayenne's expensive. So yeah. I might have nudged the officials to see things my way."

"But why lose on purpose?"

"The house always wins." Brian shrugged, as if it was obvious. "Besides, I made more money if Stadium lost. If the money's rolling in, who cares if we win or lose?"

Heather bit her tongue to keep from telling Brian he was wrong. Instead, she said, "What about the players? Did you stop to think how that might affect them?"

"There's always next year. Maybe the odds will be more profitable in Stadium's favor." He took a sip of his coffee. "It's not like they're going to amount to anything anyway. Not one of them has what it takes to play D1 ball. They're going to end up back on the farm or the ranch, living vicariously through their kids. I've got years to capitalize on this situation."

Heather cringed at his cavalier attitude. "What's going to happen when everyone finds out their beloved Coach Glover paid off the officials to make sure the team lost so that you could get a payout?"

The coach cocked his head to the side before a smirk covered his face. "Now I get it. What did she offer you?"

Heather pushed her chair away from her desk and stood up. She positioned the chair between herself and the desk. "What are you talking about?"

"Oh, come on, Heather. You're a horrible liar. Did Parker promise you a raise if you set me up?"

"You did that yourself."

Brian rolled his eyes. "Actually, I did nothing. You're the one who delivered the letters. When someone asks me what happened, I will tell them I don't know what the heck you were up to. It worked with Whittaker, and you aren't half as smart as he is. Everyone knows Matthew's business is failing and you're in debt. No one will suspect me. Whatever proof you think you have will only hurt you. Not me."

"Whittaker told the Board of Education why he really resigned. He kept records in case you came after him. He tied you to the bets in Vegas." Heather swallowed down her disgust. She'd been wrong about Brian. But now that she knew the truth, she planned to embrace it. "Even the janitor who delivered the letters for you came forward."

Brian paled, then recovered his confidence. He stood up from his chair and strolled to the door. "No one is going to believe either of those guys. Whittaker's a drunk, and Leroy's a con."

Heather let out a sigh of relief. Shannon had counted on Brian's ego to trip him up. No one in the janitorial department had fessed up, but now Shannon had the missing link. "I didn't say it was Leroy."

Brian put his hand on the door handle and shrugged. "Whatever. I don't know what you thought you were going to accomplish with all of this, but, Sugar, you've made things worse for yourself. All you had to do was keep your mouth shut. Now, I'm gonna destroy Matthew's business and make sure you won't work here next year." He turned back to her as he yanked open the door. Brian scanned Heather from head to toe and spat out, "The only good thing about Parker is she's lit. You and your stupid capris have nothing on her pencil skirts and stilettos."

"Good to know you like my attire," said Shannon in the doorway. Two sheriff's officers stood next to her. "But I'm going to have to ask you to leave the premises with these two gentlemen. We no longer need your services here at Stadium High School."

The coach pulled himself up to his full height turn thrust out his chest. "You're making a big mistake. You should haul Heather out of here. She's the one bribing people."

Shannon stepped aside and motioned for Brian to go ahead of her. "I think you'll find that I have enough evidence to prove you are the reason the Stadium High School football team lost the state championship. It would be better for everyone involved if you left without causing a scene."

Brian glared at Shannon before he took a step into the hallway. "You've got nothing on me, but I'll play your game." He turned back and looked at Heather. "You, Sugar, are going to find out what happens when you cross me."

Heather swallowed down her fear. She knew Brian couldn't do anything to her or to Matthew. In a voice calmer than she really felt, Heather said, "I'll be fine. And Brian? Never call me Sugar again."

CHAPTER 35

"**W**hat's the staff scuttlebutt?"

Heather winced as she sipped the weak tea. In the month since Shannon had escorted Brian off the school premises, Heather kept to herself. Rachel supplied her with caffeine and company, but Heather discovered Rachel's caffeine attempts didn't hold a candle to Brian's.

Rachel paced back and forth in Heather's office, her face flushed. "Strange as it sounds, no one was particularly surprised to hear what happened. Mr. Hollis had a bet about how long it would take for a new coach to be hired. My money is on Shannon pulling someone in from her old school. Makes more sense than finding someone local."

Heather couldn't help asking, "People aren't blaming me?"

"You did nothing wrong other than believe someone who you never should have listened to. But most of the staff know why and forgive you." Rachel paused and looked out the window. "Although everyone is wondering how long you are going to hide in your office."

"I'm not hiding. Just letting things get back to normal."

"Sure." Rachel turned back from the window and collapsed

into the seat. "How's it feel to be the one who brought the town's sports hero to his knees?"

Heather choked on her tea. She sputtered and coughed before catching her breath. Heather dabbed at her eyes with a tissue and croaked out, "That's a little dramatic, don't you think?"

"Accurate, though." Rachel shrugged. "The gossip brigade is impressed you stuck out your neck for the students. Mrs. Hunsinger told the Retirement Resort if they don't use Matthew for their linen service, she's calling the state to complain. Horton's turned the bed sheets all pink."

"Matthew got that business back," Heather said, then frowned. "Are you sure the teachers don't care? Sports have been king for so long, I find it hard to believe that *someone* isn't mad at me for getting the head football coach fired."

Rachel shook her head. "Heather, he did that himself. Staff are happy to have more emphasis on education. Sure, the new rules were a pain in the butt to begin with, but everything is going smoothly. The students are held accountable to a higher standard. Shannon's been a good influence, and I think most of the teachers would agree. I mean, I haven't seen a ball cap in the building for weeks. The appointment policy is divine. I miss some of the more creative artwork in the textbooks, but not once since the beginning of the year has someone said they forgot their book. The kids love the tablets. It's easy to direct them to the correct page, too. Even the attendance policy is helping. I spend less time re-teaching lessons because there are fewer absences."

"I'm not signing my contract," said Heather. The knot in her stomach loosened as soon as the words were out of her mouth.

Rachel's jaw dropped. "Way to bury the lead."

Heather shrugged and let her shoulders drop away from her ears. She didn't realize until now how nervous she'd been about announcing her decision. "I wanted your honest thoughts before I told you. Not that you can change my mind; I think it's for the best."

"Have you and Matthew discussed this?"

Heather grinned. "Several times. Including with Dr. Austen. She agreed it would be good to try my hand at something that interests me instead of doing what I've always done. The business rebounded enough that Matthew can hire back a store manager. And afford marriage counseling again!"

Rachel kicked her feet up on Heather's desk. "I say go for it. Are you going to do the college prep work?"

"Yes." Heather pushed Rachel's feet. "The school can only do so much, and I have the chance to focus on what it is I really like."

"The selfish part of me wants you to stay. Where am I going to go when I need to hide? Or complain?" Rachel winked.

"You just admitted Shannon isn't such a bad principal."

"I like how she's changed things, but you won't find me in her office any more than necessary. What did Justine say?"

"We haven't told her yet. Matthew wants to sit down with me. Going forward, it is going to be the three of us talking together. Then everyone is on the same page."

Rachel nodded her approval. "What about your mother? This might send her over the edge, don't you think?"

Heather stood up and pushed Rachel's feet off her desk before she walked to the window. "She doesn't know. She was so surprised to find out about Brian, I didn't have the heart to tell her about the job."

A knock interrupted their conversation.

"Come in," Heather called out.

The door opened, and Michael, the geometry teacher, peeked into the room and nodded at Heather and Rachel. "I don't have an appointment, but can I get a minute?"

Heather smiled and waved him into the room.

Rachel stood up. "I can leave."

Michael's face flushed when he shook his head. "No. Stay. This'll only take a minute. The faculty and staff wanted me to tell you no one blames you for anything. Coach made his own decisions, and he used you. We all know you'd never hurt the students like that. So, whenever you are ready to show up in the lounge, you're welcome. No hard feelings from anyone." He hesitated. "Well, except for Hollis. He's still bent out of shape that you didn't get the principal position. Cost him a hundred bucks."

The message surprised Heather, but she flashed Michael her best smile and said, "Thank you. I'll be in the lounge for coffee tomorrow."

Michael returned the smile with his own and left the office as quickly as he'd arrived.

"Do you believe me now?" Rachel asked. "You don't need to leave. The teachers aren't blaming you for any of this."

Heather knew then that she was her own worst enemy. If she had listened to her friends and family, she wouldn't have put herself through the discomfort of the last month. It was time to embrace her power.

"Maybe not. But I'm going to do what's better for me and Matthew this time."

Rachel sighed. "Fine. But I expect you to stop by often to bring me a good cup of coffee and a bear claw from Betty's. It's the least you could do for leaving me here at Stadium High School without my best friend."

"Deal."

"How many T-shirts do you need?"

Heather folded another shirt from Justine's collection. She wondered if she'd made a mistake not sending Justine's clothes with Matthew to the cleaners. But she wanted to spend more time with Justine before her daughter moved out of the rental house for her internship. This was one way to do it.

"Twenty. That's two weeks' worth, plus a few extras." Justine plucked a shirt from her hands. "That's one good thing from the house fire—I know exactly what I own now. Don't you have work to do?"

Heather grinned as she recognized her own words coming from her daughter's mouth.

"I do, but you're only here for a couple days. And you're spending most of that with friends. I want time with you too." She squirmed on the bed. It was time for the conversation she and Matthew agreed she would have with their daughter. "Justine, I need to talk to you."

Her daughter's face lost all its color. "Are you and Dad getting a divorce?"

"No!" Heather said, shaking her head. "Why would you think that?"

"You were sleeping in separate bedrooms last fall." The shirt Justine was folding fell out of her shaking hands. "It's my fault, isn't it? I'm the reason you don't want to be together."

Energy shot through Heather's body as she leaned forward and grabbed Justine's hands. "No divorce. We needed to work things out on our own, and that is no reflection on you. None of it was your fault. Dad and I are responsible for our own relationship."

"But if I hadn't switched majors—"

Heather pulled Justine in for a hug. "No. Our issues are ours, not yours. We're your parents, and we support you. We will always be here to love you and help you however we can."

"What if I robbed a bank and eloped with my co-conspirator?"

"Ha. Let's not test things, okay?" Heather squeezed Justine before she held her out at arm's length. "I'm your mom, and it's part of my DNA to protect you. But you are an adult. I should treat you like one. No more secrets."

Justine grinned at her before sticking out her hand. "Can we shake on that? Because I don't want to come home again and find Dot planting a sale sign in the front yard again."

"I can't promise that. But I need to tell you I didn't accept my school contract for next year. I'm going to start my own business."

Her daughter's face lit up like a sunrise. "Wow. That's amazing. What are you going to do?"

Heather explained the basics of Ramsey College Prep Services. "Your dad supports it, and the aunties encouraged me too. We'll see how it goes, but so far I'm excited for something new."

"That's amazing, Mom. I'm proud of you."

Heather felt tears come to her eyes, and she swallowed back her emotions.

Justine took her hand. "What? I can express my feelings too."

Heather waited a few seconds until she knew she could speak. "You can. But this hasn't been a banner year for me. I'm not entirely sure what you are proud of."

Justine stared back at her. "Mom, you've always stood by me. Even this year when everything hit the fan. You could have told me to stick with teaching, but you didn't. You and Dad sacrificed a lot for me." She paused, looking down at the laundry. "I'm glad you two are better."

Heather pulled her daughter into another hug. She basked in the love she had for Justine and filed away the feeling. They would argue in the future, but Heather knew she and Justine could always communicate in a way she and her own mother had only recently started doing.

She glanced at the stacks of clothes around them. "I don't suppose you'd be interested in getting rid of some clothes, would you?"

Justine laughed, and they amicably spent the next hour preparing for Justine's transition to the next phase of her college experience. Heather swallowed back a sob. Her daughter was an independent, intelligent woman who would thrive on her own. That was the thing about parenthood—when you succeeded, it still hurt.

CHAPTER 37

Heather pulled open the door to Stacey's running store. The running group always started at the park, but Stacey's text was clear:

> Change of plans. Meet at the running store.
> Don't be late.

"Hello?" Heather called out. "Where is everyone?"

"Back room." Rachel's voice carried into the store. "Hurry up. Everyone else is here."

Heather frowned. She didn't understand why they needed to meet at the store for a run, but rather than ask questions, she followed the sound of Rachel's voice. She passed through the door marked Employees Only but didn't see anyone.

A light was on in Stacey's corner office, and Heather walked toward that. She entered and was surprised to see her friends sitting on the edge of the desk. The smiles on their faces lit up the space.

"What's going on?" Heather asked as she caught sight of Christine. "You don't run. Why are you here?"

"And I never will," Christine said, "but I wanted to be here when you saw this."

The women stepped away from the desk, and Heather gasped. Hanging behind the desk was a sign announcing Ramsey College Prep Services. Bookshelves held a stack of folders with the same logo and name. A wooden chicken statue held another plaque proclaiming Expert College Advice Given Here.

Heather's knees trembled. Her heart felt full as she took in her surroundings and what her friends had done for her. Some of the tension from pursuing this new career drained out of her.

"We all contributed." Angela enveloped Heather in her arms before stepping back. "As your attorney, I've drawn up your business incorporation documents. They're ready for your signature and to be submitted to the county. I put together a list of things you need to talk to the bank about. I drafted the client intake forms and confidentiality documents. Review them and let me know if you want to make any changes. Everything is in that binder and in the documents folder on the computer."

"The computer and this office are yours for as long as you need." Stacey pointed at a conference table in the corner. "There should be enough space to work with two students at a time. Plus, you can store your marketing and prep materials here. Once you get moved back into your house, you might want to set up a home office." Stacey handed Heather a set of keys. "Until then, you are welcome to work from here."

"I'm ready and available to serve as your administrative assistant should you need one." Christine grinned at Stacey as she wrapped her arm around the other woman's shoulders. "I've already cleared it with the boss."

Rachel rubbed her hands together. "I'll refer students to you and let the teachers and counselors know you are up and running. I put together a flyer, and I'm planning to share it on a couple of the social media sites for English teachers. We should get you enough clients to make this feasible."

Heather felt her face go damp. "I don't know what to say."

"That could be a first," Rachel said.

Christine, with a laugh in her voice, said, "No, that's you who's always talking."

Stacey tapped her watch. "We have one other surprise for you.

"What else could you possibly do?"

"It isn't from us," Angela said. "It's from Shannon."

"We invited her to run today, but she's in Dallas for the weekend. She promised to join us another time, though." Rachel handed Heather an envelope. "That's a reference letter you can use with potential clients. Shannon said she would be happy to talk to any parents who want more information. She said, and I quote, 'Mrs. Ramsey is a student's best chance to getting admitted into his or her dream school and winning scholarships and grants.' The woman exalts you, even after all the crap Brian said about you."

Heather wiped her cheeks and blew out a long breath. "I don't know what I'd do without you guys."

"You're never going to find out." Angela said. "We are here for you. Always."

"Before anyone else cries, let's run," Stacey said. "There's a five-mile trail from the store I mapped out."

"This is where I say, 'Have fun,' and I'll be here working the store." Christine hugged Heather before she returned to the front of the shop.

Heather trailed the rest of the women out of her new office and paused in the doorway to look back. She could never repay her friends for this. Saying thank you would never be enough, but she understood her friends didn't care about that. They wanted the best for her. She planned to show them how successful she could be.

CHAPTER 38

Going to the gynecologist sounded more fun than calling her mother, but, like her annual exam, Heather couldn't put it off. Shannon had posted the open vice principal position. Someone was likely to see it and tell her mother. Or her mother would discover it herself when she was snooping online. Heather didn't need another Dot situation on her hands. Ruth was still milking the house sale situation.

Heather wandered outside and squinted at the sun as it lowered on the horizon. The pinkish glow sparkled from the edge of the earth, highlighting the trees and houses surrounding the area. The natural beauty of it quieted her anxiety long enough for her to dial her mother's number and sit down on the rental's front porch.

Ruth picked up on the second ring. "Hello, honey. You caught me on my way to Marge's. It's Bunco night."

"Do you ever stay home, Mom?" She rested her weight on one hand as she leaned back. Heather knew better than to pester her mother, but for some reason, the answer seemed important to her.

"It's better than sitting around in this empty house. Maybe if your dad was still alive I'd be more interested in staying home. My activities keep me young. Now, I know you didn't call to chat, so what can I help you with?"

Heather rocked forward and steadied her gaze on the sun's remaining light. "I'm not renewing my contract at the high school. I'm starting my own college prep business." Heather waited for her mother's reaction, but the line remained silent. "Mom? Are you still there?"

"Yes, of course I am." Ruth's voice sounded faint.

Hoping the shock of her decision hadn't upset her mother, Heather asked, "What do you think?"

"If it makes you happy, I'm happy."

Heather's chin fell into her free hand. "Really? That is not the reaction I expected."

"Which is my fault. If I've learned anything recently is that I should have been more supportive of you. This is your life. Make the decisions that work for you. Justine too. I wouldn't do things the same way, but that doesn't mean anything. Have some faith in yourself, Heather."

She briefly considered asking if her mother had been drinking. It seemed impossible this was her mother's actual reaction. But since her mother seemed so calm, Heather tested the waters. "What do you think Dad would think? I'm worried he'd be disappointed."

Heather winced when she heard Ruth's sigh. "Heather, your dad would be excited to know you are pursuing something you love. You've already accomplished something he would have admired."

Heather stood up and made her way inside. She slumped onto the couch as she asked, "What's that?"

"You stood up for yourself. You didn't let Brian take advantage of you."

"Technically, he did. For several years. I didn't figure it out until now." Heather settled back on the couch. She stared at the ceiling, waiting for her mother's reaction.

"Well, your dad stuck around the school *too* long. He should have retired sooner and focused on the things he liked to do. Woodworking, for example."

Heather sat up straight, and she groaned when she anticipated the next question.

But instead of asking about the Poultry Palace, Ruth asked, "Where are you planning to work from? The dry cleaners? That might be noisy for you."

The change in topic surprised her, but at least Ruth hadn't ended the call. "Stacey offered me some space in her retail store." She pressed the matter. "You're really not bothered by this?"

"No. Stop making me repeat myself. I do think you and Matthew need to have Justine take some financial courses. With all the money she'll be making, I wouldn't want her spending it on frivolous things. Speaking of which, you shouldn't buy business cards. Marge says those are a waste of time."

Heather grinned. Her mother might be able to let her make her own decisions, but she couldn't stop offering unsolicited advice.

After they got off the phone, Heather sat back on the couch and stared out the window. It was dark outside, but the call with her mother made her optimistic. If Ruth could see the good in the situation, that meant something, right?

CHAPTER 39

Heather buckled her seat belt. While she waited for Matthew to slide into the driver's seat of the car, Heather checked her new business phone for messages. She smiled at the five emails, four texts, and two voicemail messages. At this rate, she would need to take Christine up on her offer for administrative help sooner than she'd planned.

The driver's side door opened, and Matthew appeared behind the wheel. "How about some dinner? Lew's sounds good to me."

Heather frowned at the thought of returning to the restaurant where her failed promotion celebration had been held. She needed to get over it. Wasn't that what Dr. Austen said a few minutes ago at their couple's session? Forcing the smile back onto her face, Heather nodded. "Sounds better than cooking. It's lonely with just the two of us at the rental now that Justine's gone. Maybe we splurge for dessert."

Matthew backed the car out of their parking spot and headed toward the restaurant. He flicked the turn signal before navigating onto a side street. "I have an interview with a manager candidate on Thursday. Do you want to sit in on it?"

Heather lifted her eyebrows. Since they'd started meeting with Dr. Austen again, Matthew went out of his way to include her in his business decisions. For once, they were on the same page.

"That's okay. You know what you're looking for. I'll let you handle it. Christine said she was interested in the position, although I may need her." She added, "Angela has a referral as well."

"That's great. I've got a good feeling about this one, but if something happens, it's good to have options. I need to fill it soon, though. All these contracts are stretching me thin; I'm having a hard time keeping up with the admin work and the increased cleaning load." Matthew grinned at her. "Ever since Brian's extracurricular activities got out, everyone's been coming back to the cleaners."

Heather relaxed into her seat and watched the scenery out the window. Stadium was small, but it was beautiful, and it was home. Even the gossip brigade was positive lately. Heather knew that wouldn't last, but they were having too much fun talking about Brian and the drama he caused.

She frowned when they turned into Lew's parking lot. It was empty. "Well, I guess it's leftovers after all."

Matthew put the car in park and turned toward Heather. "No, Lew's expecting us." He got out of the car, meeting her at the passenger side as she stepped out.

"What's going on?"

"Your celebration dinner. It's a little overdue, but we need to make sure you can enjoy Lew's going forward." Matthew took her hand and led her to the front door. He opened it and gestured for her to enter. "After you."

Her breath hitched as the quiet hum of a string quartet welcomed her. The server from her ill-fated three-margarita night stood between a single table and a silver champagne tub. Two place settings and a small bouquet of fresh flowers rested on a white tablecloth. A white box with a turquoise bow waited next to the flowers.

Heather grasped Matthew's arm. "How did you get Lew to close the entire restaurant for us? The bowling team will boycott the dry cleaners if they find out you're the reason they can't get their post-game sliders."

"Lew and I worked out a deal. Rachel and Christine delivered the food." He led her to the table and pulled out her chair.

She caressed her husband's face and kissed him softly on the cheek. She sat down and smiled as the server presented a bottle of champagne.

"You don't need to do this, Matthew."

Heather watched as the server opened and poured the sparkling wine before disappearing back to the kitchen.

Matthew shrugged. "I do. It's been a crazy school year. Nothing turned out the way we planned. We aren't out of the woods yet, but I want you to know that we're a team, and whatever happens, we've got this." He picked up both glasses and handed her one. "To us."

The glasses clinked, reverberating throughout the empty restaurant.

"To us." Heather sipped the cold drink and sighed. "I could get used to this."

"Let's get back on our feet, then we can have champagne more often." He set down the glass and pushed the box to her. "You can open it now if you want."

She took another sip and held the glass in her hand. She twisted it in the light and watched the bubbles rise to the top. "I don't need a gift, Matthew." Heather put the glass on the table and took her husband's hand. "Our family is enough. You are enough."

Matthew chuckled. "You're right. Justine and I are over-the-top. But really. Open the box."

"Fine." She carefully removed the ribbon and peeled off the

gift wrap. Heather opened the box and pulled out a string of lights attached to a timer. She looked up at Matthew in confusion. "What is this?"

"As soon as we get settled, you can string those lights in your next chicken coop. It won't be the Poultry Palace, but it will be something that brings you new memories. I'm sorry I sold the coop. I thought it was the right thing to do."

Heather brushed her hands over the lights and waited for the longing in her chest. But the pain never came. Instead, she felt a lightness that had nothing to do with the champagne. She could leave the past behind and start fresh with Matthew.

She stood up and walked around the table. Heather pulled Matthew to his feet, drew him close, and wrapped her arms around his waist. When his lips were close to hers, she whispered, "I love you. I have always loved you. Thank you for sticking with me."

"Wouldn't have it any other way."

Their lips touched, electricity shooting through Heather's body. She trembled, excited to start anew with Matthew and turn around their lives for the better. She leaned in and enjoyed the moment.

CHAPTER 40

Heather squinted as the sun reflected off the sidewalk. She reached for the sunglasses perched on her head and gazed at the running group. Angela, Stacey, Rachel, and Shannon stretched in the parking lot. It was the first run since school let out and the first time the principal joined them. As Heather settled the sunglasses on her face, she smiled. What had started as a disaster of a school year ended better than she could ever have imagined. Old and new friends surrounded her. Matthew loved her, and her new business was off and running. She couldn't ask for more.

Heather called out to Stacey, "Thanks again for the sunglasses. They're so much better than the ones from the discount bin."

"You're welcome." Stacey finished a hamstring stretch. "They're more effective at protecting your eyes than as a head-band, though."

Heather shifted the pink frames on her face. Stacey's snarky comment didn't bother her. "What would I do without you?"

"Someone's feisty today," Rachel pointed out. She examined the neon-blue glasses Stacey had given her. "Mine are better."

The principal adjusted her black-framed glasses and nodded. "These are lovely. Thank you. I'm still amazed y'all let me join in after such a tumultuous school year."

"Glad to have you. The community hasn't been welcoming for you," Stacey said. "Makes it tough to be new."

"Not everyone's thrilled to spend time with a principal, either," Shannon said. "Especially one who helped fire the football coach."

"Their loss." Rachel looked around. "Are we going to run or just chitchat? I'm okay either way."

Heather waited for Angela's sarcastic retort, but it didn't arrive. A quick glance at her friend told her something was off. Angela's usual immaculate appearance was disordered. Her orange sport tank and yellow shorts didn't match, her purple running shoes were untied, and her hair stuck out from her head rather than corralled in her usual ponytail.

"These sunglasses were featured in last month's running magazine. Top-of-the-line." Angela turned the pair of tortoise-shell frames over in her hand. She slid them on her face before slouching down to look at her reflection in a car's side mirror.

Heather watched as Stacey jutted out a hip and raised her eyebrows at Angela. "You okay?"

"Fine." Angela's arm dropped as she bent to tie her shoes, her response stopping the conversation in its tracks.

Stacey tensed, and Heather caught her eye. Heather mimicked running, hoping Stacey got the message.

"I have a new route, so buckle up and enjoy the ride," Stacey said as she started the warmup.

Heather followed, shaking off her concern about Angela. She would share when she was ready. In the meantime, Heather soaked up the sun and the camaraderie of her friends, both old and new. She still couldn't believe how happy she was with all the changes in her life.

"Why is everyone so quiet?" Shannon asked a minute into their warmup.

Stacey looked over her shoulder. "We do the first five minutes in silence."

"Any particular reason?" asked Shannon. "It's your group, so I'm happy to comply with the rules."

"That's a good question," said Rachel. "Anyone know?"

"Tradition," Heather and Angela said at the same time, and a companionable silence fell over the women.

When Stacey's watch beeped, she asked, "What if we say something we are looking forward to next week? That might be good for all of us."

"This is a self-help group now?" Angela asked with a huff.

Heather cringed at her friend's reaction, but Stacey took it in stride. "Think of it as a full-body exercise," she explained. "I'm adding a runner's mindset class at the store. Christine and I brainstormed this question. What do you think?"

"I'm new here, but I like it. It's dual-purpose. A person acknowledges her goals and connects to others who might help or are in a similar position," Shannon said, then added, "I should add something like that to the staff meetings next year."

"I'm game," said Rachel. "Both here and at school. Could be nice to get to know my fellow teachers better."

"I like it, too, especially since I'll be flying solo next year. Encouragement's a good thing." Heather looked over her shoulder at Angela, who trailed behind the group. She expected her friend to chime in, but Angela seemed lost in her own world. "Ange, what do you think?"

Angela looked up and shrugged. "I prefer the silent running tradition."

"What's up with you?" called out Rachel.

"You asked what I thought, and I told you." Angela slowed to a walk, letting out a long exhale.

The rest of the group skittered to a stop around her. Heather wondered if her face looked as worried as everyone else's did. Nothing usually bothered Angela, but the attorney was troubled.

"Sorry. Work sucks," Angela said, her voice shaking. "I can't talk about it other than to say I look forward to not having to babysit a new associate. All help is not good help."

Shannon nodded. "I've dealt with my fair share of teachers who've been problematic. It's not the same thing, but sometimes people don't understand the mess they create for others."

Heather surveyed the group, taking in looks of surprise and curiosity on the other women's faces. She half-expected Rachel to ask if one of those teachers was her ex-husband.

Stacey waved everyone forward, effectively changing the topic. "Hey, we need to pick up the pace. Exercise releases endorphins, and endorphins—"

Only Rachel and Heather chimed in, "Boost your mood."

"Not sure I can run fast enough," muttered Angela, and the group picked up where they left off.

Heather resisted the urge to comfort Angela and let the warm spring air whip past her. She finally understood the importance of taking control of her own life. Her turnaround had given her the chance to reclaim her relationships with Matthew, Justine, and her mother and strengthen her friendships. Without the chaos of the last year, she wouldn't have had the courage to start something new.

Heather couldn't help herself and blurted out. "Change is good!"

Four heads turned toward her.

"Never did I think that Heather Ramsey would embrace the new," Stacey said.

Rachel nodded. "Is there a full moon?"

"She's fine. She's evolving. Isn't that we're supposed to do?" said Angela.

Shannon chimed in, "I don't know about y'all, but I'm doing

whatever I want these days. I don't have anyone to answer to, but even if I did, I wouldn't change a thing."

The comment caught Heather off guard. "Me too."

Angela said in a winded voice, "We noticed. You're more relaxed than I've seen you in years. Maybe decades."

"I wonder if that's because of us or because of Matthew," Rachel said.

Heather's face felt hot, and it wasn't from the running. "I'm relaxed. Let's leave it at that."

A phone chimed, and everyone reached for their phones. Angela blanched at whatever she saw and said, "I've got to go back to the office."

"If I knew it was that easy to get out of a run, I would have offered extra credit to a student to text me," piped up Rachel.

Shannon shook her head. "I'll pretend I didn't hear that."

Angela gave everyone a quick hug before turning around and retracing her steps.

"Don't forget to stretch," Stacey called out. "That's part of the run!"

"Yeah, yeah," Angela waved back. Heather's stomach clenched as she watched her friend, but she knew Angela could handle whatever work could dish out.

"Does that happen a lot?" Shannon asked as the four of them continued their progress.

Stacey shrugged. "Sometimes. It's not typical."

"Don't worry about her," Rachel said. "I want to know who Shannon found to replace Brian."

As much as Angela's departure bothered her, Heather gave in to Rachel's distraction. A lively debate ensued about new football coaches. They speculated about whether Mrs. Hunsinger would ever stop gossiping. Everyone, including Shannon, spitballed ideas to promote Ramsey College Prep Services. Satisfaction and pride filled Heather, and she basked in it as she continued running with her friends.

EPILOGUE

$\mathcal{A}$ngela sprinted back to the parking lot. She put as much distance between herself and her friends as possible in case she got another text.

Or worse—a phone call.

She entered the parking lot, slowed to a walk, and stopped next to her car. Angela bent over, her hands on her knees, gasping for breath. The sprint should have drained her anxiety and embarrassment. Instead, it left her tired, sweaty, and on the verge of a headache.

When Nicole popped back up in her life a decade ago, Angela welcomed her. It comforted her to have someone around who witnessed the most traumatic part of her life. Her running friends knew about the decision she made in law school and supported it. Nicole experienced it.

But somewhere along the way, things changed. Angela didn't know what caused the transformation. Maybe it was Nicole's series of questionable jobs, her four failed marriages, or the alcohol and drugs the woman indulged in. Angela only knew that Nicole morphed from the helpful, generous friend into a manipulative extortionist.

Angela's phone beeped again, and she jerked in surprise. She dropped her car keys, and they clattered under her vehicle. Annoyed with herself for letting things make her nervous, Angela closed her eyes and took a deep breath before reading the text.

> Have you decided? It's not like you don't have the money.

Ignoring the sender didn't do any good. She'd tried that, but Nicole didn't get the hint. This time, Angela used common sense.

> Money isn't the answer. Get yourself clean. Then we'll talk.

She stuffed the phone into her pocket and reached down to pick up her keys. Angela gasped as a sharp pain shot from her hamstring up through her lower back. She hated when Stacey was right. Neglecting to stretch wasn't a good idea.

Gingerly, Angela stood up and opened her car door. She carefully slid behind the steering wheel and drew her legs inside. Her body didn't like the position, but it complied. She wiped away the sweat dripping from her forehead, unsure if it was from the run or the pain in her back.

The phone chirped again as she started the engine. Angela hooked up the phone to the car's hands-free system and backed out of the parking spot before listening to the text. She almost rear-ended the car in the spot across from her when she heard Nicole's response.

> I'm calling Robyn now.

Panic swelled in her chest, and Angela swerved back into her parking spot. This was exactly why she had left the run. Nicole's threats had become more erratic lately, and Angela worried the woman would follow through on her threats.

It took less than ten seconds to transfer the money Nicole demanded. This sort of thing used to happen every two or three years, but in the last year, it had escalated. A quick glance at her banking app told Angela it was the third time this year, and it was only May. She knew she made the situation worse by giving in, but she didn't feel like she had an option. Not if she wanted to protect Robyn.

Angela didn't care if the world knew about the baby she gave up for adoption while she was in law school. It couldn't hurt her now. Most of her partners and associates harbored their own skeletons deep in their wine cellars.

It was Robyn's life she was concerned for. Her daughter deserved to make her own choices, and if she didn't want to know who her biological parents were, that was her decision. Nicole forcing that information on Robyn was wrong.

Leaning back on the headrest, Angela wondered if she should get in touch with Robyn's father, Gregory. After they agreed to give the baby to a couple who were ready to be parents, she and Gregory broke up. But even if Angela got ahold of him, Gregory might not want to talk about it.

Tossing her phone into her passenger seat, Angela decided to figure things out on her own. She turned the car back onto the road and drove to the office. She'd planned to go home and shower, but she didn't deserve that. If she couldn't stand up to Nicole, then maybe she deserved to be blackmailed.

WANT MORE?

Want to know how Shannon found her way to Stadium High School? Read *Back Around,* a Running with Friends *free* bonus short story.

Get *Back Around* at https://BookHip.com/VRGPMZK

Because sometimes a detour is exactly what you need to find your way.

ABOUT THE AUTHOR

Carole Wolfe writes women's fiction that makes you smile. She enjoys running at a leisurely pace, crocheting baby blankets for others and drinking wine when she can find the time. After moving nine times in twenty years, Carole and her family have settled in Texas.

Follow Carole at www.carolewolfe.com.

ALSO BY CAROLE WOLFE

WOMEN'S FICTION TITLES

My Best Series

My Best Mistake - Tasha's Story

My Best Decision - Sara's Story

My Best Memory - Helene's Story

My Best Gamble - Brianna's Story

My Best Break - Cynthia's Story

Running with Friends

Turn Around

CHILDREN'S TITLES

Sneaky the Pudge Weasel Series

Goodbye with a Smile